Tales from the
Arabian Nights

The Most Famous Stories from the Great Classic

A THOUSAND AND ONE NIGHTS

Told by Margaret Soifer and Irwin Shapiro

Illustrated by Gustaf Tenggren

GOLDEN PRESS · NEW YORK

C-1

SECOND PRINTING

Contents

Scheherazade or The Story of These Stories

MANY YEARS AGO, King Shahriar ruled over the land of Arabia. He lived in a splendid palace, where glittering fountains filled the courtyards with tinkling music. His storehouses were heaped high with rare and precious treasures. He had a wife whom he loved dearly, and many slaves to carry out his smallest wish. He should have been one of the happiest men in the world.

And so he was, until one day he found his wife plotting against him. He had her put to death at once, but still his rage was not satisfied.

"No woman can be trusted," he said.

Each day he ordered his Grand Vizier to bring him a beautiful young woman for a bride. The King married her at a fine wedding. Then, the very next morning, he had her beheaded. Day after day this went on, until there was hardly a family in the city that had not lost a daughter.

Of all the unhappy people in the city, the unhappiest was the Grand Vizier. It was his duty to find a new bride for the King every day—and to see that she was beheaded the next morning. To make it worse, he himself had two daughters. Many people grumbled behind his back, saying, "He has eyes for our daughters, but is blind to his own."

Now the elder of the Grand Vizier's daughters was named Scheherazade. Besides being good and beautiful, she was learned and wise.

"Father," she said to him, "you must let me be the next bride of the King."

"What!" gasped her father. "Shall I lead my own child to her death?"

"I have a plan," Scheherazade said. "If it succeeds, we will save the city."

"And if it fails?"

"Then things will be no worse than they are now. Father, I beg you to let me try."

When the Vizier saw that he could not change her mind, he took her to the King.

"Foolish man!" the King said, frowning. "Do not expect mercy from me because she is

9

your own daughter. You know my custom."

Before her father could answer, Scheherazade said, "It was my wish to be your bride, O King, not my father's."

"Then let the marriage take place," said the King. "But remember—you will die tomorrow, as all my other brides have died."

"I understand," said Scheherazade. "But may I ask one small favor? I have a younger sister whom I love dearly. I would like her to spend the night in the royal palace, so that I may kiss her farewell tomorrow before I die."

"You ask little enough. You may send for your sister," the King said.

And so the sister, Dunyazade, came to the palace. Then Scheherazade and the King were married. When the bride kissed her father, she whispered to him, "Do not lose hope, dear father." And when she kissed her sister, she whispered, "Do not fail me, little one. Remember well what we planned."

"I will remember," Dunyazade said. And, two or three hours after midnight, she knocked at the door of the royal chamber. The King threw open the door.

"What are you doing here at this hour, little sister?" asked Scheherazade, pretending to be surprised.

"Oh, dear sister," Dunyazade said, "I have been lying awake, thinking of you and how you are about to die. I have been thinking, too, of the wonderful tales you tell, and which you will tell no more. Would you tell me a story now to remember forever and ever?"

"If the King will permit it, I should like nothing better than to spend my last hours telling a story," Scheherazade said.

The King gave his permission, and Scheherazade began to tell a story. At dawn she had just reached the most exciting part. To hear how the story ended, the King was forced to put off her beheading until the next day.

That night, as Scheherazade continued her story, she wove another right into it. At dawn, the King was again left wondering how it would end. Again he had to put off Scheherazade's death.

This went on day after day, week after week, month after month, year after year, for a thousand and one nights. In that time, the King forgot his sorrow and his wish for revenge. Because of Scheherazade, he lost his distrust of women. Little by little, he had come to love her, for her beauty and goodness, her wisdom and skill.

In this book are set down some of the tales told by Scheherazade, during those thousand and one enchanted Arabian nights.

Aladdin and The Wonderful Lamp

IN A great city of China, there once lived a widow and her only son, Aladdin. Their home was a poor little hut in a poor and crowded part of the city.

All day Aladdin's mother scrubbed and cooked and spun flax into thread for a few miserable pennies. Although he was fifteen years old, Aladdin did nothing to help his mother. He roamed the streets and the bazaars, returning home only for supper. And yet his mother never scolded him. She loved her son, and was sure that some day he would be a great and wealthy man.

One day, as Aladdin was playing with some boys in a street far from home, he noticed a stranger watching him. The stranger was tall, and he had a long, thin, drooping mustache. He was dressed in rich, foreign-looking clothes.

When Aladdin started for home, the stranger quickly followed him. He soon overtook Aladdin and began asking all sorts of questions. His manner was kind, and Aladdin answered truthfully, hiding nothing. Indeed, Aladdin had so little to tell that there was nothing to hide.

At last the stranger asked, "May I come home with you and share your evening meal, Aladdin?"

"Yes, if you like," said Aladdin. "But I don't know if you will get enough to eat. I never do."

"That is easily taken care of," replied the stranger. They were passing through a bazaar, and he bought bread, fruit, roast duck, pastries, and wine. The two reached Aladdin's home with their arms full of delicious things to eat.

Aladdin's mother hardly knew what to think of the tall, beautifully dressed stranger. She liked his fine manners. And she was glad to have all that food, for she had not had a good meal in years. But somehow, although she could not have told why, she did not trust the man.

Perhaps it was his smile that troubled her most. Framed in that long, thin, drooping mustache, it seemed too wide and full of teeth. And so she kept her eyes on him, and was careful not to say too much.

After they had eaten and the table had been cleared, the stranger began talking earnestly.

"I am your poor husband's elder brother," he said.

"But my husband had no brothers!" the widow said in surprise.

"Then he must never have told you about me," said the stranger sadly. "I was twenty years older, and left China to seek my fortune when he was only a little child. And now to think that he is dead!" And he sighed and wiped a tear from his eyes.

"Where have you been all these years?" asked the widow. She half believed the story, in spite of her uneasiness.

"I wandered over the world for a few years until I came to Africa. There I made my fortune," the stranger said. He looked down at his fine clothes and the rings which flashed on his fingers. "After forty years, I suddenly became homesick. I wanted to leave my fortune to my own flesh and blood. I came back here, but could not find our house. The whole neighborhood where we lived seemed to be gone. I walked about the streets for days. Suddenly, today, I saw Aladdin. He looks exactly as my brother did when he was a child."

He put his arm affectionately around Aladdin's shoulder. "I shall make him my heir. And you, my dear sister-in-law, need work and starve no more!"

The man seemed to mean what he said, for after that he visited Aladdin and his mother every day. He brought them food, or gave them money for clothes and furnishings for their house. He was especially nice to Aladdin, whom he called "nephew." Soon the boy wore silks, as though he were a young mandarin. And very handsome he looked in them, too.

One day, the new-found uncle came to Aladdin's home at daybreak. He explained that Aladdin must go with him on an important errand. Hustling the sleepy boy into his clothes, he led the way out of the city. They followed a road to the foot of a great mountain, where there stood a mighty, jagged rock.

The man told Aladdin to help him gather twigs for a fire. They worked quickly, and soon a small but fierce fire was burning and crackling. Taking a small box out of his wide sleeve, the man sprinkled black powder on the fire. At the same time, he spoke some magic words.

The jagged rock began to move, and slowly toppled over on its side. Where it had stood, a flight of stone steps led down, down, down into the earth. Quickly the stranger, whom Aladdin now knew to be a magician, spoke to him.

"Go down those stairs," the magician said. "When you come to a door, open it. Walk quickly through three rooms. The first will be filled with jars of copper money, the next with silver, and the third with gold. Do not touch a single coin, or you will die at once. The money is the treasure of the genii, and they guard it well.

"Next you will come to a garden filled with trees laden with fruit-shaped jewels. There you will see an old lamp lying on the ground. Take the lamp and return to me as fast as you can, because the rock will not wait. The magic spell has moved it aside for only a few moments. Hurry now! Hurry!"

"How do I know I will be safe, dear uncle?" asked Aladdin, trembling and afraid.

"Here is my ring," the magician said impatiently. "Put it on your finger. It will keep you from all harm if you hurry."

Aladdin put the ring on his finger, and the man almost pushed him down the stairs.

Everything was just as the magician had said. Aladdin was too frightened even to look at the pots of money in the three rooms. He ran into the garden, picked up a dirty old copper lamp that lay on the ground, and turned to leave.

Suddenly he heard a delightful tinkling sound. A breeze was rustling the branches of the trees, on which grew beautiful fruit-shaped jewels. There were emerald pears,

14

ruby apples and cherries, and peaches of opal. Aladdin stopped to pluck a few of each kind, putting them in the hidden pockets of his wide sleeves. Then he hurried back through the rooms to the flight of stairs.

"The lamp! Throw me the lamp!" the magician shouted down to him.

"As soon as I come up, dear uncle," said Aladdin.

"Throw it up to me now, you filthy little slave!" cried the man, forgetting all his fine manners. For the earth was trembling, and soon the rock would return to its place.

"Oh, uncle, pull me up before it is too late!" said Aladdin, starting up the stairs.

"First throw me the lamp! The lamp!" shouted the frantic magician.

But Aladdin kept running up the stairs, trying to reach the top. Already the rock was slowly moving. Then there was a great trembling of the earth that sent him flying to the bottom of the stairs. With a rumble, the rock settled back into place, cutting off his escape.

For a while, Aladdin lay there, stunned. At last he opened his eyes and looked around in the dim light. Now he understood the magician's scheme. The wicked man had made up the whole story about being his uncle, just to get him to fetch the lamp. Aladdin knew the magician had never meant him to come up into the sunlight again.

For a long time Aladdin thought of all the hours he had spent in idleness. If only he could have another chance, he would make something of himself. But what was the use of thinking about that now? Soon, in this dim place within the earth, he would die of hunger and thirst.

Crying and sobbing, Aladdin sank down upon his knees. As he clasped his hands to pray, he happened to rub the ring on his finger—the ring the magician had given him. The next minute a tremendous genie stood before him, roaring:

"What is your will, O Master?"

More frightened than ever, Aladdin managed to ask, "Who are you?"

"I am the Genie of the Ring," the monster said. "I serve him who rubs the ring."

Picking up the lamp, Aladdin said at once, "Then get me out of this place!"

In a wink it was done.

Out in the sunlight, Aladdin rubbed the ring again. Again the genie appeared.

"Set me down before my mother's house," ordered Aladdin. Before the last word had left his lips, Aladdin stood before the house.

Aladdin's mother wept with joy over his safe return. When she heard his story, she blamed herself for trusting the wicked stranger.

"Dry your tears, mother," Aladdin said, "and let us have some food."

The widow sighed. "Alas, we have not even a crumb left in the house. Perhaps if I polish up this old lamp, I can sell it at the bazaar."

But no sooner had she begun to rub the lamp, than a huge genie rose up in the room.

"What is your bidding, O Master of the Lamp?" the genie asked.

The widow fainted. But Aladdin, who had already seen a genie, stepped forward.

"Bring us something to eat," he said.

The genie vanished, returning in a moment with a table loaded with choice foods. There were roast meats, fruits, tarts, wines, all served on silver dishes. The smell of the food soon brought the mother out of her faint. She and Aladdin sat down at the table, eating until they could eat no more.

The food that was left over from the feast lasted them for many days afterward. When it was gone, Aladdin sold one of the silver platters. He received enough money to keep him and his mother in food for weeks—and he still had many more silver platters.

Early one morning, while Aladdin was in the bazaar, soldiers came clattering down the street. They ordered all the people into their homes. The Princess would soon pass by, and no one was allowed to look at her.

Filled with a great curiosity to see the princess, Aladdin stepped behind a door. He left it open just a crack, and peered out. As

16

the Princess came by in her jeweled palanquin, she drew aside her veil for a moment. Aladdin caught only a glimpse of her face, but it was enough. Never had he seen anyone so beautiful.

After the Princess had gone on, Aladdin ran all the way home.

"Mother," he said, "I am in love with the daughter of the Emperor! Please call on him and tell him I wish to marry the Princess!"

The poor woman thought that Aladdin had a fever and did not know what he was saying.

"How am I to do that, my son?" she said quietly, hoping to calm him.

Her eyes grew wide as Aladdin showed her a handful of the fruit-shaped jewels he had gathered in the underground garden. He had kept them hidden, but now he put them on a platter and covered them with a silken cloth.

"Take these jewels as a gift to the Emperor," he said, "and tell him of my great love for his daughter."

That very morning Aladdin's mother went to the royal palace. All day she waited in the great hall where the Emperor held court, but no one noticed her. Day after day she went to the palace, waiting patiently to be brought before the Emperor.

At last, after a month had passed, the Emperor said to his Vizier, "Who is that poorly dressed woman who comes each day with a covered dish?"

The Vizier brought Aladdin's mother before the Emperor, and she uncovered the dish. How amazed the Emperor was to see the sparkling jewels, each the shape and size of a piece of fruit!

"These are a gift to you from my son," Aladdin's mother said. "It is in this manner that he asks for the hand of your daughter in marriage."

"He must be a man of great power and wealth," said the Emperor, greedily fingering the jewels.

But why, he wondered, would a wealthy man's mother go about so poorly dressed?

Winking slyly at the Vizier, the Emperor said, "I shall indeed be happy to have my daughter marry your son. But first he must build her a palace in the royal garden. When it is finished, you may come to me with your son, and the marriage will take place."

As the widow knelt and touched her head to the ground, the Emperor and the Vizier laughed aloud.

Leaving the palace, the widow hurried home to Aladdin.

"Oh, my son, my son," she said, "they made fun of you before the whole court!"

Aladdin did not seem at all worried.

"What did the Emperor say?" he asked.

"First, he took the jewels. Then he said he would allow the marriage if you built a palace for his daughter in the royal garden. Then he looked at the Vizier, and both of them laughed."

"Good, good!" said Aladdin.

He took the wonderful lamp from the cupboard and rubbed it. At once the genie stood before him.

"What is your will, O Master?" said the genie in his deep, rumbling voice.

Aladdin answered, "Build a palace in the royal garden to match the beauty of the Royal Princess. The walls are to be of solid gold and the windows framed with jewels. The furniture is to be of ebony, ivory, and teakwood, carved and encrusted with jewels. The dishes must be of gold and alabaster.

There must be barns and stables, with coaches and fine horses. A carpet of beautiful design and a canopy of shining satin are to lead from the Emperor's palace to the new home of the Princess. And you may put in the palace anything else you think fitting. When all of this is done, return to me."

The genie disappeared. Aladdin drew a long breath—and the genie was again standing before him.

"I have done as you asked, O Master," the genie said. "Servants are already at work in the palace, preparing the wedding feast."

"Good!" said Aladdin. "Now dress my mother and me in rich clothing. Bring me a hundred soldiers, fully equipped and mounted on horses. And roll out a carpet that will lead from this hut to the palace."

Aladdin's mother was still a pretty woman, and in her new clothes she looked like a queen. Aladdin himself, looking every inch a prince, took his place at the head of the soldiers. As they were about to start for the palace, he turned to the genie.

"Genie," he said, "give each of my men a pot of small gold coins, to scatter among the crowds as we ride by."

Aladdin put his wonderful lamp in the wide sleeves of his tunic. He helped his mother up on a gentle white horse, mounted a handsome black charger, and started for the palace. Everywhere people ran out of their houses to see the procession. They cheered and screamed with joy as they scrambled for the shining coins flung out to them on all sides by the smiling soldiers.

The Emperor and his Vizier heard the shouting and came out of the palace to see what was happening. They were astonished to see the marvelous palace that had sprung up in the royal garden. Where had it come from? Then the gay procession came into view, and the Emperor greeted Aladdin.

The Emperor was so pleased with Aladdin and the palace that he consented at once to the marriage. When the Princess was brought to Aladdin, she immediately fell in love with him. And, after much feasting and merrymaking, they settled down to a happy life together in their golden palace.

Everywhere the wonderful story of the Princess's marriage was told. At last it reached the ears of the wicked magician who had sent Aladdin for the lamp. He had returned to Africa, a disappointed man. When he heard the name of the young man who could build a palace in the wink of an eye, he knew that Aladdin had escaped from the cave and learned the secret of the lamp.

Now the magician hurried back to China, where he did nothing but watch Aladdin's palace. Then, one day, he saw Aladdin set out from the palace with a hundred horsemen. The Emperor had asked his son-in-law to deliver a message to a neighboring king.

This was the chance the magician had been waiting for. He put on the clothes of a peddler and flung a sack of cheap, shiny lamps over his shoulder. Walking close to the golden palace, he called out:

"New lamps for old! I sell new lamps for old! New lamps for old!

A silly servant girl popped her head out of a jeweled window.

"Oh, peddler!" she called. "Do you mean to say you will give me a bright new lamp for an old, tarnished one?"

"Indeed I will, my lady," said the magician, smiling and bowing low.

"Wait here!" the girl said.

Running to her master's room, she snatched up the old lamp that stood on a shelf.

"The Prince and the Princess will be delighted when they hear of this," she thought.

She gave the old lamp to the smiling magician, who gave her a new one in return. As soon as she was back in the palace, the magician rubbed the old lamp. The genie immediately appeared.

"Take me, this palace, and all that are in it to Africa!" commanded the magician, and the genie obeyed.

When Aladdin returned home with his horsemen, the Emperor rushed out to him.

"Gone, gone!" cried the Emperor, wailing and wringing his hands. "Your palace, the Princess—everything! Gone, gone!"

Aladdin wasted no time in wailing or wringing his hands. Instead, he carefully questioned the Emperor's servants. He soon

21

found out that a peddler with a long, drooping mustache had been near the palace, selling new lamps for old. And he knew this could only be the wicked magician who had once pretended to be his uncle.

Quickly Aladdin rubbed his ring, and the genie appeared before him.

"Bring me back my palace and all that are in it!" Aladdin said.

"That I cannot do, O Master," said the genie. "The palace is the work of the Genie of the Lamp."

"Then set me down before my palace," said Aladdin, and at once he was in Africa.

He hid until a servant whom he trusted came to one of the palace windows.

"Take me to your mistress," ordered Aladdin.

Aladdin and the Princess embraced, then made a plan. Aladdin slipped out of the palace, returning later with some sleeping powder he had bought. That night, while Aladdin hid, the Princess secretly put the powder in the magician's wine.

As soon as the magician fell into a deep sleep, Aladdin rushed out of his hiding place. The magician always carried the wonderful lamp in his wide sleeve, and there Aladdin found it. He rubbed the lamp, and the genie stood before him.

"Take this palace and all of us back home," Aladdin said. "But destroy this wicked magician, so that no more may he seek to destroy others."

In a moment the palace was back in China, where Aladdin and the Princess were greeted joyfully by the people. From that time on, Aladdin and the Princess lived happily in their golden palace. As for the magician, no one knew what had become of him. But never was that wicked man seen on earth again.

Ali Baba and The Forty Thieves

LONG AGO, in a city of Persia, there lived a poor woodcutter named Ali Baba. He and his brother Kassim had each been left a little money by their father. But Kassim had married a rich wife and had become a wealthy merchant. Ali Baba had married a poor wife, and his money was soon gone. Now it was all he could do to support his family by going into the forest and cutting firewood to sell.

Late one afternoon, Ali Baba was at the edge of the forest. He had finished his work for the day. His three donkeys were loaded with firewood, and he was ready to set out for home. Suddenly he heard the pounding of horses' hoofs. Across the plain, in a cloud of dust, a band of horsemen was galloping toward him.

Fearing that they might be robbers, Ali Baba quickly tied up his donkeys in a

thicket. Then he climbed a tree, to hide in the branches until the horsemen rode by.

To his amazement, they stopped before a huge rock not far from the tree. Fierce-looking men they were, too, with scimitars in their belts. Before Ali Baba could wonder what was in their bulging saddlebags, their chief cried out:

"Open, Sesame!"

And the great rock slid aside, showing the mouth of a cave. So wide was the cave that the horsemen could enter two abreast. There were forty horsemen in all, including the chief. When they had disappeared inside the cave, the rock slid back into place.

Up in the tree, Ali Baba wondered what to do. Should he climb down and try to get home? The horsemen might come out at any moment and capture him.

Ali Baba decided to wait for a while. It was a good thing he did, for the great rock moved aside again and the horsemen came out, all forty of them. Then the rock moved back, sealing up the cave.

As soon as the horsemen had galloped away, Ali Baba clambered down from his tree. Standing before the rock, he called out in a bold voice:

"Open, Sesame!"

He was delighted to see the rock obey his command. He stepped inside the cave, and the rock moved back, closing off the mouth of the cave. Even so, enough light came from an opening in the roof for him to see. And what a sight lay before him! There were huge bags filled with glittering gold. There were enormous jars overflowing with blazing jewels. Costly silks and rugs were strewn about in careless heaps. Never had he even dreamed of such a rich

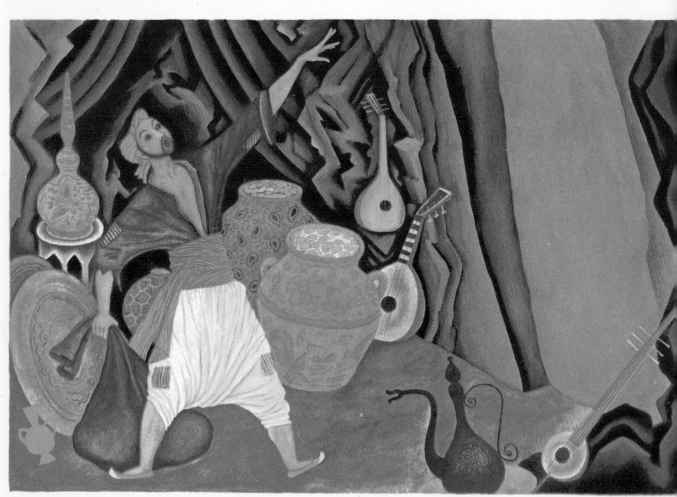

treasure. Surely the cave had been used as a
storehouse by thieves for many years.

Quickly Ali Baba took off his worn cloak.
He filled it with gold and jewels, tying it
up with the sleeves.

"Open, Sesame!" said Ali Baba.

Again the rock obeyed. Ali Baba stepped
out of the cave, and the rock closed behind
him. He hurried to his donkeys, dragging
the cloak on the ground, for it was much
too heavy for him to lift.

Working as fast as he could, Ali Baba took
the firewood out of the sacks on his donkeys' backs. He loaded the sacks with the
gold and jewels. Over the sacks he laid some
wood, so that no one could see that he had
made his fortune that day.

It was late at night when he entered the
courtyard of his home. His wife opened the
door for him.

"Are you all right?" she asked. "I was
sure something terrible had happened!"

"Sh!" Ali Baba said, putting his finger on
his lips. "Come and help me."

When the treasure was safely inside the
house, he told her the whole story. She
listened hungrily to every word, her eyes
sparkling like the gold and jewels heaped up
on the table and the floor.

"If the thieves learn of this, we will surely
be murdered," Ali Baba said. "We must
bury everything under the floor. Help me,
wife—but hurry!"

"Can't we count our treasure before we
hide it?" the wife said. "Wait—I know a
quicker way! I'll borrow a measuring cup
from our sister-in-law, and we can measure
the amount of our riches!"

And she ran next door, to the house of
Ali Baba's rich brother Kassim. Kassim was
asleep, but his wife fetched the measuring
cup. Curious to know what Ali Baba was

measuring, she rubbed the inside of the cup
with a bit of fat. And when the cup was
returned a little later, a gleaming gold coin
was stuck to it.

Kassim's wife ran upstairs and shook her
sleeping husband by the shoulder.

"Kassim! Kassim! Wake up!" she cried.
"Your brother is always complaining about
how poor he is—and here he spends the night
measuring out gold pieces!"

Holding out the gold coin, she explained
what had happened. Wide awake now, Kassim put on his clothes and hurried to his
brother's house. There he found Ali Baba
and his wife replacing the bricks in the floor
over the gold and jewels. Kassim demanded
the truth about the treasure, and Ali Baba
told him everything.

"In the morning I will take ten donkeys
and visit the cave myself," Kassim said.

"Be careful, brother," Ali Baba said. "It
will be worth your life if the thieves discover you."

Kassim sneered. "I do not need your advice, my dear brother," he said.

Kassim slept little that night. In the first gray light of the morning, he set out for the cave. Ali Baba had told him where to go, and soon he found the rock.

Tying his ten donkeys to the trees, Kassim called out:

"Open, Sesame!"

And the great stone moved aside.

Inside the cave, Kassim almost went out of his mind with greed. Gold was not enough for him. He dragged priceless rugs and tapestries from their places along the walls. He spent many minutes looking at the jeweled crowns, belts, and daggers, trying to choose those with the largest gems.

At last he was ready to leave. He had only to repeat the password, and the rock would slide back from the mouth of the cave.

But what *was* the password? He remembered that it was the name of some grain or herb or seed. But in his excitement over the treasure he had forgotten the exact word.

"Open, Barley!" he said — but nothing happened.

"Open, Rye! Open, Caraway! Open, Fennel! Open, open, open!" he cried, beating his fists against the rock.

Then from the outside came the clatter of horses' hoofs, and Kassim trembled with fright. The thieves were returning. He ran to the back of the cave, where he hid behind some bales of silk.

Peering out, Kassim saw the rock move aside. The forty thieves entered, their scimitars in their hands. They had seen Kassim's donkeys tied to the trees. While two of the thieves stood guard at the door, the others began to search the cave.

Kassim slipped from one hiding place to another, but the thieves soon saw him. He ran for the door, only to be stopped by the guards. The thieves' scimitars flashed, cutting Kassim's body into quarters.

Inside the entrance, the thieves hung

what was left of Kassim, as a warning to anyone who might discover their secret. Then they rode off, driving Kassim's donkeys with them.

All that day Kassim's wife waited for him to return. When night came, she ran to Ali Baba, crying and wringing her hands. She demanded that Ali Baba look for his brother at once. Ali Baba tried to quiet her.

"Perhaps Kassim has lost his way in the darkness," he said. "If he has not returned by morning, I will look for him."

In the morning, of course, there was still no sign of Kassim. Taking his donkeys, Ali Baba went to the thieves' cave. As soon as the rock slid aside, he saw what had happened. He wept as he took down the pieces of his poor brother's body and wrapped them in cloths. He put them on the donkeys' backs, together with several bags of gold, covering everything with firewood. Sadly he turned his steps toward home.

Now in the house of Kassim there was a slave girl named Morgiana. She was not only loyal and brave, but very wise as well. To Morgiana Ali Baba went, and told her the whole frightful story.

"You must keep your mistress quiet," he said. "We must make it look as though Kassim died a natural death. Otherwise the thieves will kill us all."

"I understand, good master," Morgiana said. "Do not worry."

Morgiana saw to it that her mistress remained in an inner room, where her cries of grief could not be overheard by the neighbors. The next day, Morgiana rose at the first glimmer of dawn. Wrapping herself in a large black shawl, she hurried to the Street of the Leatherworkers at the edge of the city. Here she found one lone old man already at work.

"There is at my master's house a very delicate job of leatherwork," she said to the

old man. "It requires a good eye, a steady hand, and a stout heart."

And Morgiana put a heavy gold piece on the table before the old man.

He said, "That I have a good eye is proved by the fact that I am already at work in this dim light. That I have a steady hand, you can see by the samples of my work around you. That I have a stout heart you can prove by putting me to the test."

"There will be another piece of gold for you when you finish," Morgiana said. "But first I must blindfold you."

She tied a heavy silk scarf over his eyes and led him through the sleeping town to Kassim's house. The blindfold was removed, and the man was given the task of sewing together Kassim's body, so that it could be clothed for burial. When he was finished, Morgiana paid him and blindfolded him again. She led him through the streets, and he was back in his shop before the people of the town were up and about.

Later that morning, Morgiana tore her clothes, put ashes on her head, and went to the market to do the shopping. She wept and wailed, telling everyone that Kassim had just died of a stroke. And when the funeral was held the next day, no one suspected that he had not died in that way.

Since Kassim and his wife had had no children, all his wealth went to Ali Baba, who moved into his brother's fine house. Kassim's widow became part of Ali Baba's household, and his son took over Kassim's business. Ali Baba began to live the easy life of a wealthy man, sometimes going to the bazaars to buy or sell a precious jewel.

But there was trouble in store for him. The next time the forty thieves returned to their cave, they saw that Kassim's body was missing. It was plain that someone knew how to enter the cave. Their treasure would not be safe until they had killed the man who knew their secret. And so one of the thieves disguised himself and set out to find their enemy.

The thief reached the city at daybreak, before it was really light. Quietly he walked along the Street of the Leatherworkers. Only one shop was open, and in it an old man was at work. The thief stopped to chat with him, just to pass the time.

"You must have sharp eyes to work in so little light," the thief said politely.

"Not at all," the old man said. "You should have seen what I had to do in even less light than this."

"What did you do, may I ask?"

"I had to sew together a man's body that had been cut into four pieces!"

"Where was that?" asked the thief eagerly. "I'll give you a gold piece—and a heavy one—if you can show me the place!"

"I was taken there blindfolded," the old

man said. "Blindfold me again, and I will probably remember how I was led."

The thief was overjoyed to think that he had come upon the right man at his first try. At once he blindfolded the old man, who walked straight to Ali Baba's house.

"This is the house I entered," the old man said. "Now give me my gold piece."

The thief handed him a coin. Then he took a piece of white chalk from his pocket and marked an X on the house.

Later that morning, when Morgiana came out of the house to do some shopping, she noticed the chalk mark. She went back inside and came out again with a piece of white chalk. She marked the houses on both sides of the street with an X, then calmly did her shopping.

When the thief returned to the street with the rest of the band, he could not point out the right house. Enraged, the chief ordered him beheaded.

"Who else will now try to find the house of our enemy?" the chief asked. "Ten bags of gold to him if he succeeds! But if he fails, he will die!"

And so another thief tried. He, too, went to the old man, who brought him to Ali Baba's house. The thief marked it with red chalk. But Morgiana noticed the new mark, and marked all the houses on the street in just the same way. Again the thieves failed, and again one of their band was beheaded.

Now the chief decided to seek out the house himself. But he made no chalk marks. Instead, he carefully memorized the location of the house. Then he went back to the forest to make his plans.

A few days later, a little after sunset, the chief rode up to the house of Ali Baba. He was disguised as an oil merchant, and had with him nineteen donkeys. Each of the donkeys carried two great oil jars.

"Kind sir," said the chief to Ali Baba, "I have traveled far today, and my donkeys are tired. If you will allow me to stay the night, I will pay you well. See, I have fine oil to sell."

And he opened one of the jars, which did indeed contain olive oil.

"This is not an inn, my friend," said Ali Baba kindly. "But you are welcome to stay as my guest."

"You are most generous," the chief said.

The donkeys were led into the courtyard, where a servant helped to unload the huge, heavy oil jars. They were placed in a neat row, and the donkeys were fed and bedded down for the night. Then the guest was given a room overlooking the courtyard.

This was exactly as the chief had planned. For only one of the thirty-eight jars contained oil. Hidden in each of the rest was a thief. Later, in the middle of the night, the chief would throw a handful of pebbles into the courtyard. At this signal, the thieves would climb out of the jars and put to death everyone in Ali Baba's house.

But it was still early in the evening, and all was peaceful. While Ali Baba chatted pleasantly with his guest, Morgiana prepared dinner in the kitchen. Noticing that her cruet of olive oil was empty, she thought she would refill it from one of the many jars lined up in the courtyard. She went out in the dark and lifted the lid of the nearest jar. To her surprise and horror, she heard a man say in a whisper:

"Is it time?"

Morgiana understood at once what was going on. Making her voice as deep as she could, she whispered:

"It is not yet time."

Morgiana went from jar to jar, getting the same question and giving the same answer. She filled her cruet from the only jar that contained oil, then went back into the house to serve dinner.

As soon as she could leave the dining hall, Morgiana filled all the kettles in the house with oil from the big jar. She put the kettles on the fire until the oil was boiling hot. Then she carried the kettles out to the courtyard and carefully poured boiling oil into each of the jars. The thieves were smothered before they could even cry out. When she was finished, Morgiana went back into the house and lay down to sleep.

It was well past midnight before the chief was sure that the household was asleep. Quietly he opened his window and threw out some pebbles. They rattled on the flagstones in the courtyard—but no one came out of the jars.

After a few minutes, the chief tried again. Again he waited. At last he stole out of the house to find out why his men had not answered the signal. The moment he lifted the lid of the first jar, he knew. Filled with rage, he climbed over the courtyard wall and hurried back to the forest.

The next day, Ali Baba was surprised to see the donkeys and the oil jars still in the courtyard. Even more strange, there was no trace of the merchant. Then Morgiana told Ali Baba why the merchant had run away. Tears came to Ali Baba's eyes as he heard how the brave, quick-thinking girl had saved his life and the lives of his family.

"Morgiana, you are no longer a slave," he said. "You are now free to do as you wish— but I do not know how I will get along without you."

31

"I am happy to be free," Morgiana said. "But I will go on serving you, if you will allow it." For she still feared the chief of the thieves, and wanted to remain with the family to watch over them.

The thief, all alone as he was, could think of nothing but revenge. For days he watched Ali Baba's house from a distance. He discovered that Ali Baba's son went out early every morning. Following him, he found where the young man had his shop. In a few weeks, the thief opened a shop of his own nearby, filling it with precious things from his cave. The false merchant then made friends with Ali Baba's son. He was so kind and charming that soon the young man could talk of nothing else.

"Bring him home with you some evening," said Ali Baba, and his son did.

Now the thief had dyed his hair and grown a beard. He had changed his way of dressing and speaking. Neither Ali Baba nor his son suspected who he was. But wise Morgiana knew him at once, when she came into the dining hall with a tray of fruit. And when she bent close to serve him, she saw the handle of the dagger which he kept hidden in his robe.

As soon as dinner was over, and the men were having coffee, Morgiana spoke to Ali Baba. "May I have your permission, master, to dance for your guest?"

"What a delightful idea!" said Ali Baba, for Morgiana was a fine dancer and singer. "You may, indeed."

Morgiana left to put on her dancing costume. She was back in a few minutes, two jeweled daggers in her hands. To the sound of a tambour played by a slave boy, she danced, the daggers flashing as she spun and whirled. The men watched, spellbound by her beauty. Suddenly, at the wildest moment of the dance, she leaped at the thief and drove a dagger straight into his heart.

Horrified, Ali Baba cried out, "What have you done? Have you lost your mind, Morgiana? We are disgraced forever!"

"No, dear master," answered Morgiana, "you are not disgraced. You are saved. Look carefully and you will see that your guest was the chief of the thieves. Here is the dagger with which he was going to stab you."

Ali Baba saw the dagger, and peered closely at the thief.

"Ah, wise Morgiana," he said. "I have already given you your freedom. Is there anything else I can do to show how thankful I am?"

"May I ask something of you, dear father?" spoke up Ali Baba's son. "For many months now, Morgiana and I have known that we love each other. Will you give us your permission to marry?"

"Gladly!" said Ali Baba. "You could not have chosen a better wife!"

And so, in time, the wedding was held, and there was feasting and merry-making. And for years and years, whenever anyone in Ali Baba's family wanted some of the world's riches, he had only to go to a certain rock in the forest and call out:

"Open, Sesame!"

The Caliph and the Cucumbers

ONE MORNING, the good Caliph Maan Ben Zaideh went hunting with a band of merry companions. As the huntsmen entered the royal forest, the Caliph spied a deer. Away he rode after it, going so swiftly that he soon left all his companions far behind.

After a hard chase, the Caliph lost sight of the deer. But he was not troubled. He got down from his horse and, since it was a pleasant day, he sat under a tree. He was spattered with mud, and had torn his hunting clothes while riding through the thickets. This, too, did not trouble the Caliph. He hummed a tune and looked happily around, for it was not often that he could enjoy the pleasure of being alone.

Then he heard the cloppety-clop of a donkey's hoofs on the path that led through the forest to his palace. In a few minutes, a farmer came shuffling along. He was leading a donkey whose saddlebags were crammed with cucumbers.

The Caliph was amazed.

"Good morning, friend," he said. "May I ask where in the world you are going with all those cucumbers?"

"I am going to the palace, to sell them to the Caliph," replied the farmer proudly.

"And where did you get cucumbers at this time of year?" the Caliph asked. "Surely they are out of season."

"Indeed they are," the farmer said. "You see, I come from the district of Cuzah, where, as you may know, we have had a drought for two years. Well, this year it started to rain, so I planted cucumbers—hundreds of them. And behold, they sprang up weeks before their time! So I gathered all my donkey could carry, and now I will sell them to the Caliph."

"But why to the Caliph, may I ask?"

"For two reasons," the farmer said. "First, only a caliph will pay a proper price for vegetables out of season. Second, the Caliph Ben Zaideh is famous for being free with his money."

The Caliph solemnly nodded his head.

"Indeed that is so. And how much will you ask the Caliph for your cucumbers?"

"A thousand dinars," the farmer said.

The Caliph jumped up. "A thousand dinars! But that is too much! Suppose the Caliph refuses to buy them for a thousand dinars?"

"Then I will ask for five hundred," the farmer said.

"Ah! I see. And suppose he refuses to pay five hundred?"

"Three hundred, then."

"Surely you can't ask three hundred."

"Two hundred."

"Still too much," said the Caliph, shaking his head.

"Very well, then. One hundred," the farmer said.

By now the farmer was beginning to feel

35

sorry for himself. He sighed. "You really think a hundred dinars is too much? Maybe I'll ask for fifty."

"Suppose he refuses to pay fifty."

"Then I'll be a poor man," the farmer said. "Thirty dinars."

"And if the Caliph will not give thirty?"

The farmer flew into a rage. "Then I'll—I'll—I'll take my donkey and leave him right on the carpet where the high and mighty Caliph sits on his throne! A caliph who won't pay a poor man thirty dinars for cucumbers out of season does not deserve respect!"

It was all the Caliph could do to keep from bursting into laughter.

"Do not disturb yourself so, friend," he said quickly. "The Caliph may yet give you a good price, and all will be well."

Slowly the farmer's anger faded, and the smile came back to his face.

"These are good cucumbers," he said. "And they really are out of season. Besides, everyone knows the Caliph is generous. "

"Well, good fortune, friend. May your journey be prosperous," said the Caliph.

And he swung himself upon his horse and galloped off, waving good-by. When he arrived at his palace, his servants helped him prepare for his appearance at court. At last, bathed and dressed in the royal robes, and wearing magnificent jewels, he went into the chamber where he held court.

He called his chamberlain to him and said, "If there is a farmer with two saddle-bags of cucumbers waiting to see me, admit him at once."

The farmer was soon brought in. Naturally, he did not recognize the Caliph as the hunter he had met that morning.

After bowing the correct number of times, the farmer said, "Your Highness, knowing how much you like cucumbers, especially when they are out of season, I have come all the way from Cuzah with the finest from my garden."

The Caliph turned to his chamberlain. "Let me see one of those out-of-season cucumbers," he said.

The farmer took a cucumber out of one of the bags and handed it to the chamberlain. The chamberlain gave it to the Caliph, who sniffed it and fingered it expertly.

"And how much do you want for your

cucumbers, my good man?" the Caliph asked the farmer.

"A thousand dinars, Your Highness," the farmer answered.

"A thousand dinars? Ridiculous! Take them away!" And the Caliph waved his hand.

"Will five hundred please Your Highness, then?" the farmer said quickly, watching the Caliph's face.

"Indeed not. I'll not pay such a high price for cucumbers, in or out of season."

"Shall we make it three hundred, then?"

"No. That's still too much," the Caliph said. "Far too much."

"But Your Highness," the farmer said, "you may graciously remember that we have had two years of drought in Cuzah. These are the first vegetables I've had from my garden in all that time. Will you buy the cucumbers for two hundred?"

"Am I buying cucumbers or am I giving alms?" the Caliph said, pretending to be angry. "I will certainly not pay two hundred dinars for ordinary cucumbers."

"One hundred dinars—surely you will buy them for one hundred! I carried them all the way from Cuzah. . . ."

The Caliph shook his head. "Is it the distance or the cucumbers you are selling? No, not one hundred!"

"Fifty?" asked the farmer.

"No, not fifty!" cried the Caliph. "And not thirty, either!"

"Not even thirty?" Suddenly the farmer realized who the Caliph was. "In that case," he said, his face red with embarrassment, "my donkey is—is safely tied outside."

A great shout of laughter burst from the Caliph. He laughed until all the court laughed with him. He laughed until the farmer had to laugh, too. He went on laughing until even the donkey tied outside laughed with a loud hee-haw.

When at last he could speak again, the Caliph said, "I will buy your cucumbers, my friend, and I will give you all you asked for them." He turned to his chamberlain. "Give this man a thousand dinars, five hundred dinars, three hundred, two hundred, one hundred, fifty, and thirty!"

The chamberlain quickly added up all the sums. He paid the farmer two thousand, one hundred and eighty gold dinars.

The farmer went home a rich man, and the good Caliph—well, he ate cucumbers for two weeks after!

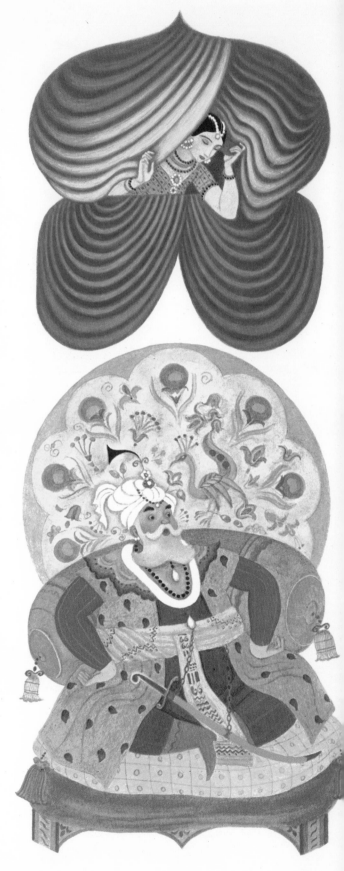

38

The Magic Horse

KING SABOUR seemed to have everything in the world that a man could wish for. The kingdom over which he ruled stretched farther than he himself had ever traveled. His wife was beautiful, kind and wise. His three daughters were the loveliest and most talented young ladies in the kingdom. He had a son who was brave, handsome and manly. He had mighty armies, and palaces full of gold and jewels, with delightful gardens where the murmur of fountains could be heard all day long.

And yet King Sabour was not content.

He was always seeking rare and costly things which would make him talked about and envied.

And so it was that one day three magicians, attended by their servants, came to his palace. They were bearded and strange-looking men, dressed in robes embroidered with curious signs.

The magicians told the guards at the gate, "We come from the ends of the earth, and we have brought with us extraordinary gifts for the King."

"Bring the magicians before me," said the King. "If their gifts are truly extraordinary, I shall be glad to give them whatever they wish in return."

Leaning forward on his throne, he waited to see what the strangers had to offer.

The magicians were brought before the King, and the first one stepped forward. At his command, his servants displayed the statue of a soldier, of gold encrusted with jewels. In the soldier's golden hand was a golden trumpet.

"What is so extraordinary about this statue?" asked King Sabour, raising his eyebrows. "It looks quite ordinary to me."

"Your Majesty," the magician answered, "this statue can stand guard over your palace night and day. Just place it on the gatepost. If an enemy should try to enter at any time, the golden soldier will lift his trumpet to his mouth. He will blow a blast so loud and clear that your entire army will hear it and come running."

The King clapped his hands with delight, for no one else in the world had such a magic statue. But he put a stern look on his face.

"We must test your statue. If it does as you say, what would you like in return?"

"That is easily answered," the magician said. "The beauty and goodness of your oldest daughter are known everywhere. I wish to have her as my bride."

Now, in those days, it was the custom for fathers to decide whom their children would marry. And King Sabour was so anxious to get the golden trumpeter that he did not stop to think whether the magician would be a good husband for his daughter.

Instead, he said quickly, "It shall be as you wish. If the statue is everything you say, you may wed my oldest daughter."

Then the second magician signaled to his servants, and they brought forth a huge silver bowl. In the center of it was a golden peacock. And all around the rim perched twenty-four chicks, skillfully fashioned.

"But what is so extraordinary about this bowl?" asked the King.

"This work of art," the second magician said, "is a clock. On every hour, the peacock pecks one of the chicks, flaps its wings, and calls out the time of day. And—most wonderful of all—at the beginning of each month, the bird opens its beak and shows the new moon in its throat."

The King eyed the bowl greedily. "These wonders you tell about are easily tested. What do you wish in return for this gift?"

"Your Majesty," the magician said, "the loveliness and talents of your second daughter are known throughout the world. I beg for her hand in marriage."

"Very well," said the King. "You shall marry her as soon as this bowl proves its magic powers."

Now the third magician came forward. His servants placed before the King a life-sized horse, carved from shining ebony. With its saddle, bridle and stirrups all dazzling with jewels, it was a marvel to behold.

"Am I a child?" said King Sabour, sneering. "Are you offering me a toy?"

"No, indeed, Your Majesty," said the third magician. "There is not, and never will be, another horse like this in the whole wide world. This horse will take its rider through the air anywhere he wishes to go."

"A flying horse!" gasped the King.

"Yes, a flying horse—gentle, safe, never growing tired, never growing old. I can teach Your Majesty how to ride him any time you like."

"Good! Good!" the King said. "And what do you want in return for the horse?"

"Wherever I have gone in my travels," said the third magician, "I have heard of the beauty of your youngest daughter. I wish to marry her."

"And so you shall!" cried the King. Jumping up from his throne, he stroked the wooden horse and admired its trappings.

Now it happened that King Sabour's youngest daughter was hiding behind the curtains that hung at one side of the throne room. More curious than her sisters, she listened eagerly to everything that was said. When she heard herself promised in marriage by her father, she parted the curtains just enough to get a glimpse of the man she was to marry.

What she saw almost made her fall in a faint. The magician was at least sixty years old. He was toothless and none too clean, and on his face was a mean, sour expression. How could her father be so blinded by a gift, no matter how extraordinary, that he would give his own daughter to such a creature? Sobbing bitterly, she ran through the corridors of the palace toward her room.

Before she could get there, the Prince, who was her brother and the only son of the King, came walking by.

"Who has brought tears to the eyes of my beloved little sister?" he asked.

41

"Our own father!" she cried. "I must find some way to die before my marriage, for our father has just promised me to the most hateful creature I ever saw!"

The Prince asked his sister a few more questions, then promised to do what he could to bring their father to his senses. He found the King in the courtyard examining the horse, together with the magician and a crowd of courtiers.

"Father!" said the Prince. "Are you exchanging my sister for a wooden horse?"

"But this is a magic horse, my son," the King said, and turned to the magician. "Show my son how to ride this marvel."

The magician saw at once that the Prince was not greedy like his father. It would be best to get rid of him quickly.

"Mount the magic horse, O Prince," he said, bowing low, "and if you please, I will show you the wonders of this creature."

Impatiently, the Prince leaped into the saddle.

The magician said, "Guide the horse in the direction you wish to go by pulling on the reins, as if it were alive. Now, do you see the ivory knob to the right, below the horse's neck? Turn that and you will rise."

Following the magician's instructions, the Prince turned the knob. The horse rocked on its legs, and the crowd moved back to make room. Slowly, the horse rose into the air. Higher and higher it went, carrying the Prince with it. The crowd watched, fascinated, until horse and rider were nothing but a speck in the sky. Then the King spoke to the magician.

"Now bring my son back," he said.

The magician smiled and bowed. "That I cannot do. But I can create for you another magic gift, equally deserving of your daughter's hand."

"I want my son back at once!" roared King Sabour.

"He cannot return, O Sire," the magician said. "Unwisely, he did not wait to find out how to make the horse come down."

King Sabour stared at the magician. Suddenly he realized how greedy and foolish he had been.

"Take back your gifts," he said to the first two magicians. "Leave my kingdom immediately!" He ordered his guards to put the third magician into jail, and to keep him in chains until the Prince returned.

"Your son will never return!" cried the magician as he was being led away.

"Then you will die!" the King said.

Rushing to his own rooms, he tore his clothes, sprinkled ashes on his head, and mourned for his son. Soon the palace, and then the city, and then the entire country

enough so that he could watch for a good place to land and spend the night.

At last the Prince saw a beautiful city glimmering in the dusk. He circled around it until he came to the towers of a spacious palace. Since he did not know whether strangers were welcome in this land, he brought his horse down on the palace roof. He would spend the night under the stars.

"I can be thankful for at least one thing," thought the Prince. "My horse can do without hay or grain. I will start back for home at the first sign of day."

He lay down and tried to close his eyes. But he had not eaten all day, and he was too hungry to sleep.

"Perhaps I can find something to eat in the palace," he thought.

Opening a door in one of the towers, he quietly stole down the steps. He could see nothing in the darkness, and no one seemed to be stirring. But after going down four flights of stairs, he saw a soft light.

The Prince walked toward the light, and clapped his hand over his mouth to keep from laughing. Stretched out on the floor, before a curtained doorway, lay a guard. He was the largest and ugliest man the Prince had ever seen, and he was snoring loudly in his sleep. Near him were the remains of a fine supper.

The Prince lost no time in helping himself to meat, bread, fruit and sweets, while the guard snored on. Then he stealthily picked up the huge sabre that lay at the sleeping man's side. Parting the curtain over the doorway, he stepped into a magnificent chamber. By the dim light of a few candles burning in a corner, he saw a canopied bed with the curtains drawn.

The Prince tiptoed to the bed and gently drew aside the curtains. He gasped, for in

was in mourning. The once happy land became a place of gloom, while King Sabour wept for his son and blamed himself for his great misfortune.

Meanwhile, the Prince had been journeying through the air, riding the magic horse. At first he had enjoyed racing through space with the swiftness of an eagle. But now, as he left his own country behind and saw strange mountains, forests and seas below him, he wished to turn back. He turned the knob a little, but the horse only flew higher. And when he tried to turn the knob the other way, nothing happened.

"Surely," the Prince said to himself, "if there is a knob for going up, there must be another knob for going down."

Carefully he felt the neck of the horse under its silken mane, and there, toward the left, he found another knob. He turned it just a little. To his great relief, the horse began to go down. The Prince did not bring the horse all the way down, because he was flying over a vast sea. But he did fly low the bed lay the most beautiful girl he had ever seen. As he stared at her, she slowly opened her eyes and looked up at him.

"Are you a dream, or are you real?" she asked softly.

"I am no dream, Your Highness," answered the Prince, rightly guessing that the girl was a princess. "I am a stranger in your land, but I mean no harm."

His words awoke the Princess's hand-maidens, who had been sleeping in the room. They sat up, listening as the Princess questioned the Prince. The two young people sat and talked through the night. Hour after hour went by, but to them it seemed as though only a few minutes had passed.

Suddenly, when it was almost dawn, the huge guard rushed into the room. He had awakened to find his sabre gone, and had come to see if the Princess was safe. To his

amazement, he saw a stranger sitting beside her. With a roar of rage he sprang toward the Prince to kill him with his bare hands. But the Prince leaped up and brandished the sabre.

"Come one step closer," cried the Prince, "and I will slice off your head."

The guard drew back, knowing how sharp was the blade of his own sabre.

He said, "I will tell the King that a stranger has broken into his palace and is in the private chamber of his daughter!"

"All is well, guard," the Princess said. "Go call my father, and tell him that I wish to speak to him."

The guard rushed out. He was back in a minute with the enraged and sleepy King, who was ready to kill the man who had broken into his palace and ruined his rest.

"Sire," the Prince said respectfully, "I am truly sorry that I have come to you as an intruder. But I knew nothing of you or your people, and was afraid that you might not welcome strangers. Now that I have learned to know your lovely daughter, may I tell Your Majesty that I am the son of King Sabour of Persia. I love your daughter and ask permission to marry her."

The King shook his head. "If you had come honorably to my gates and asked in a straightforward manner to marry my daughter, I would have been delighted. You are a fine-looking young man, and I have heard of the wealth of your father. But since you broke in at night like a thief and won my daughter's favor before you came to me, I cannot give my consent."

"Then may I fight for the Princess's hand?" asked the Prince.

"Young man," the King said, "for what you have done, I should order you thrown into prison and executed. But I can plainly see by my daughter's face that you have won her favor, so you shall be allowed to die honorably in combat. Whom do you choose to fight?"

"Your entire army, if it please Your Majesty," the Prince said.

The King could not help smiling. "I have forty thousand men. Will you fight all of them at once?"

"Yes," answered the Prince boldly. "And I hope to win the Princess, who is dearer to me than my own life."

"It shall be as you ask," the King said. "You shall face my entire army at sunrise, and they will be ordered to show no mercy."

And he left to dress and to give his troops their orders. The Prince hurriedly whispered something to the Princess, then went down to the courtyard.

Soon he saw the King's soldiers assembling in a nearby field. In row after row they came, riding their fine horses, looking fierce and splendid with their shields and lances. Before long the palace door opened, and out marched the King with his viziers, courtiers, and servants.

"Bring the stranger a suit of armor and a good horse," the King commanded.

"Your Majesty is indeed kind, but I will use no armor, and I will ride my own horse."

"Where is your horse?" asked the King.

"On the palace roof," the Prince said.

A shout of laughter rose from those who were standing close enough to hear him. His words were repeated and passed from one person to another, until every one of the forty thousand soldiers was laughing.

Obeying the King's orders, some servants went to the roof. They came back carrying the beautiful wooden horse. The King stared at it, astonished.

"Do you intend to meet your death on this?" he asked.

"Your Majesty," the Prince said, "it is on this horse that I intend to conquer. Will it please Your Majesty to ask your men to stand back fifty paces, so that I may have a fair chance?"

After the men moved back, the Prince leaped into the saddle of the magic horse. With the reins he turned it in the direction of Persia. Then he twisted the right knob a little. To the amazement of everyone, the horse swayed and started to rise.

"Come, my beloved!" called the Prince, and the Princess ran to his side. He swept her up into the saddle and turned the knob. The horse soared into the air and went flying swiftly toward Persia.

Reaching the kingdom of King Sabour, the Prince turned the knob to bring the horse down. Later, many people said they were the first to see a tiny speck rushing toward them from the sky. But no matter who saw it first, the speck grew larger and larger until anyone could see that it was the Prince on his magic horse, bringing with him a strange, lovely princess from a strange land. Hastily the King brushed the ashes from his clothes and the royal family prepared for the wedding. Once again Persia was a happy land.

Some days after the wedding, the Prince spoke to his father.

"My beloved wife is pining for her home," he said. "She is her father's only child, and she thinks of how sad he must be now that she has fled from him. Tell me, my father—how can she let him know that she is happy in her new home?"

King Sabour remembered his own sadness when his son had disappeared on the magic horse.

"You and your lovely wife must visit her father at once," he said.

"But how shall we travel?"

"Have you forgotten the magic horse? It is safe in my treasure house."

"Father," the Prince said, "you must give back the horse to the magician who brought it here. I will not make my sister unhappy for any gift, no matter how wonderful."

King Sabour nodded. "You speak wisely, my son. I, too, have learned that there is nothing more precious than the happiness of our loved ones. But when you were carried off so suddenly because of the wicked plot of the magician, I had him put into prison. Then I could not rest until I had him beheaded. You can see, therefore, that there is no sense in not making use of the horse, for he has no other master but you."

"Yes, father," the Prince said.

And from that time on, the Prince and the Princess flew back and forth from one country to another, whenever they pleased. And great was the joy of their families and the people of their lands, because of their devotion and goodness.

The Sleeper Awakened

ONCE there was in Baghdad a young man named Abou Hassan, who was left a fortune by his father. He put aside half of his wealth to live on, and the other half he spent on entertaining his friends. In a year or so this half of his money was gone, and his friends would have nothing more to do with him.

"Ah," he said, "how ungrateful men are! From now on I will be friends with no one. I will pass the time with strangers, and I will be careful to see them only once."

And so Abou Hassan sat every evening

48

at the bridge over the Tigris River. When he saw a stranger he would take him home, where the two would talk pleasantly over a good dinner and fine wines. And in the morning Abou Hassan would send the stranger on his way, never to see him again.

One evening he was at the bridge when the Caliph Haroun al-Raschid, who ruled over Baghdad, came walking by with a servant. The Caliph was going about the city disguised as a merchant, which was his custom. In this way he went among his people and found out how they lived.

Not knowing who the Caliph was, Abou Hassan invited him to his house. The Caliph went willingly enough. He enjoyed the dinner and the wines, and, even more, he enjoyed Abou Hassan's company.

"Tell me, my young friend," he said, "is there anything I can do to repay your kindness?"

Abou Hassan thanked him, but shook his head. "There is nothing I wish from you—nor, indeed, shall we ever meet again." And he told the Caliph why he never entertained anyone more than once.

"I see," the Caliph said. "But are you sure there is nothing I can do for you?"

"Nothing at all. I am perfectly satisfied with my life the way it is," Abou Hassan said. "There is one little thing, though, that troubles me. I have four neighbors, all old men, who speak against me. Every day, for no reason at all, they spread all sorts of tales about me. People like that should be punished. If I could be Caliph for one day, I would have them paraded around the city in rags. I would order a crier to go before them, shouting, 'This is the punishment for mischief-makers who spread false tales about their neighbors!'"

The Caliph smiled. He had just thought of a way to help Abou Hassan and amuse himself at the same time. But all he said was:

"Come, my young friend! Let us have another cup of wine!"

Filling Abou Hassan's cup, he secretly dropped a sleeping powder into it. No sooner had Abou Hassan drunk his wine than his head rolled, his eyes closed, and he fell asleep.

The Caliph called to his servant, who had been waiting outside.

"Put this man on your back," he said, pointing to Abou Hassan, "and follow me."

The servant did as he was told, following the Caliph through the dark streets to the palace. Here the Caliph had Abou Hassan undressed and put into his bed. Then he called together everyone in his household—the Grand Vizier and the other officers, the guards and servants, and the ladies of the court.

"When this sleeper awakes," he said, "tell him he is the Caliph—and treat him as such. Carry out all his orders, no matter what they are."

After giving a few more instructions, the Caliph went to sleep in another part of the palace. The next morning he hurried to the room where Abou Hassan was still lying in bed. The Caliph hid himself in a small closet, leaving the door open a crack so that he could peer out and see what happened.

Soon, following the Caliph's instructions, the Grand Vizier entered the room. With him were servants of all kinds, and ladies of the court. They had not long to wait before Abou Hassan opened his eyes.

Astonished, Abou Hassan looked around at the magnificent room. He stared at the walls and ceiling, inlaid with gold. He stared at the silken curtains over the doors,

at the soft carpets, and the furniture, and the vases of gold and porcelain and crystal. He stared, too, at the people who bowed before him.

"I must be dreaming a dream," he murmured, and closed his eyes again.

"O Caliph, it is time for Your Majesty to arise," the Grand Vizier said.

Abou Hassan's eyes opened wide, and he sat up in the bed.

"What did you say?" he asked, amazed. "Who am I?"

"You are the Caliph, Your Majesty," the Grand Vizier said.

"I do not seem to be asleep," said Abou Hassan slowly. "And yet I cannot be awake. For how could I become Caliph in one night?"

As he looked around again, bewildered, servants brought him a gold basin and a

silver pitcher of water for washing. They clothed him in robes of fine silk and linen, put the Caliph's royal dagger in his hand, and led him to the throne room.

"I must be the Caliph," he said. "This cannot be a dream, for all these things do not happen in a dream."

And he sat down on the throne, while all about him the people of the court bowed low.

"Now that I am Caliph," Abou Hassan thought, "I can deal with my neighbors."

He ordered that his four neighbors be paraded around the city in rags, seated backwards on camels. A crier was to go before them, shouting, "This is the punishment for mischief-makers who spread false tales about their neighbors!"

"It shall be done, O Caliph," the Grand Vizier said.

"Then, when they have been paraded around Baghdad, have them sent to another city, never to return," Abou Hassan said.

"Also go to the home of a certain Abou Hassan, and give his mother one hundred gold dinars."

After attending to all the business of the court, Abou Hassan spent the rest of the day feasting and merry-making. Meanwhile the real Caliph kept himself hidden. He laughed as he watched Abou Hassan, greatly enjoying the joke he had played. When darkness came the Caliph whispered to a servant to put a sleeping powder in Abou Hassan's wine. Abou Hassan soon fell asleep. His own clothes were put back on him and he was carried to his own house.

The next morning Abou Hassan was awakened by his mother.

"Who are you?" he asked sleepily. "And where am I?"

"I am your mother and this is your house," answered his mother.

"Do not lie to me, woman," Abou Hassan said. "For I am the Caliph!"

His mother gave a little shriek and

clapped her hand over his mouth. "Have you lost your mind? Be quiet, my son! What if the Caliph should hear of this!"

Looking around, Abou Hassan saw that he was indeed in his own house. Sighing and shaking his head, he told his mother what had happened.

"It must have been a dream, after all," he said, sighing again. "Or else that merchant I brought home was a magician who cast a spell over me."

"Whatever it was, you had better forget about it," his mother said. Suddenly she smiled. "Oh, I have good news for you, my son! You know the four neighbors who troubled you with their tales? They were paraded around the city and sent away from Baghdad for good. And the Caliph sent me a gift of a hundred gold dinars."

"What!" cried Abou Hassan. "Now I know that I am really the Caliph, and did not just dream! It was by my orders that those four men were punished! And it was I who sent you the hundred dinars! I tell you, I am the Caliph!"

And he shouted and roared and cried out until his mother had to get a physician to quiet him. For several weeks he lay in bed. Slowly he gave up the idea that he was the Caliph, and was sure that he had been under a magician's spell.

At last, after a month had passed, Abou Hassan wished to entertain someone at dinner. And so he went to the bridge to wait for a stranger. He had been there only a little while, when who should come by but the Caliph! Again the Caliph had but one servant with him, and again he was disguised as a merchant.

"Ah, Abou Hassan! How good to see you, my young friend!" the Caliph said, embracing him.

Abou Hassan pushed the Caliph away. "I have no greeting for you, O merchant, nor do I want yours! You cast a spell over me—and after I entertained you in my house!"

"A spell? I?" said the Caliph. "Come, come! Surely you must be mistaken. But let us eat and drink together, and you will tell me exactly what happened."

"No," Abou Hassan said, frowning. "Why should I speak to someone who caused me so much trouble? Besides, you know it is my custom never to entertain a stranger more than once. So just be on your way and leave me alone."

But the Caliph would not go. Unable to get rid of him, Abou Hassan shrugged his shoulders and took the Caliph to his house. They ate and drank, and soon were talking together like the best of friends. The Caliph could hardly keep from laughing as Abou Hassan told him what had happened.

"This is a strange tale," the Caliph said, pouring wine into Abou Hassan's cup. At the same time he dropped a sleeping powder into it.

Abou Hassan swallowed his wine, and a moment later he was asleep.

"Carry him to the palace," the Caliph said to his servant.

This time Abou Hassan was not put to bed, but was laid gently on a couch. At the Caliph's command, servants and ladies of the court gathered about him. They sang and played lutes and flutes and tambourines, while the Caliph hid behind a curtain.

Awakened by the music, Abou Hassan opened his eyes.

"Am I going mad?" he said. "Or has a spell been cast over me again?"

He covered his face with the sleeve of his robe, as though to shut out the sight of the splendid palace and the sound of the music.

A servant bowed and said to Abou Hassan, "Arise, O Caliph, and look upon your palace and your faithful servants."

Abou Hassan sat up. "Who am I?" he asked. "Who am I?"

And a lady of the court answered, "The Caliph, Your Majesty."

"You lie!" said Abou Hassan. Then, holding out his hand, he said, "If I am the Caliph, bite me, so that I will know whether I am awake or asleep."

"As you command," the lady said, and bit his finger.

Crying out with pain, Abou Hassan jumped to his feet.

"This is no dream!" he shouted.

A great burst of laughter came from the ladies and the servants. They danced around Abou Hassan, singing and playing their instruments. Abou Hassan joined in the dance. He jumped and leaped and whirled and kicked his heels.

Watching from behind the curtain, the real Caliph laughed until tears flowed from his eyes. He thrust the curtain aside and came into the room, saying:

"Enough! Enough, O Abou Hassan, or you will kill me with laughter!"

At once the singing and the dancing stopped, and everyone bowed low.

"We await your command, O Caliph," said a lady of the court.

"You!" Abou Hasssan said. "The merchant I entertained in my house! You are the Caliph!"

"Yes," said the Caliph.

He explained how he had tricked Abou Hassan, then gave him silken robes and a thousand gold dinars and other fine gifts.

After that Abou Hassan was always made welcome at the palace, and spent many hours with the Caliph, feasting and merrymaking. Before long he married a beautiful lady of the court, and, enjoying the Caliph's friendship, lived in happiness to the end of his days.

IN THE time when Haroun al-Raschid was Caliph of Baghdad, there was a poor porter who carried heavy loads from one part of the city to another. One hot day his load was even heavier than usual. Tired and miserable, he sat down on a marble bench that stood beside the gate of a magnificent house.

As he rested, from the house came the sound of sweet music, and the rich smell of wines and roast meat and other delicious things.

"Ah," the porter said bitterly, "they feast and make merry here—but I must tramp the streets with my burdens from morning till night."

And he made up some verses and recited them aloud:

> *How good to rest here in the shade!*
> *Yet soon—too soon, I am afraid—*
> *I must pick up my heavy pack*
> *And carry it on my weary back.*
> *For I must work, in cold or heat,*
> *Just to get a bite to eat,*
> *While some, who never lift a hand,*
> *Live in ease on the fat of the land.*
> *Tell me, now, why must this be,*
> *When they are only men like me!*

Slowly the porter got to his feet. But before he could lift his pack, a servant opened the gate of the house.

"Come," said the servant.

And he led the porter inside to a tall man with a gray beard.

"I am the master of this house," the tall man said, "and I am called Sinbad the Sailor. I could not help hearing your verses through the window."

Fearful and ashamed, the porter said, "I meant no harm, my lord!"

Sinbad smiled. "Do not be afraid. I liked your verses. But I want you to know that I became wealthy only after much trouble and many dangerous voyages upon the seas. Now sit down and have dinner with me, and you shall hear my story."

"Gladly," the porter said.

And, while food was brought to them on gold and silver dishes, Sinbad began the tale of his strange adventures:

My father was a rich man, and when he died, he left me his entire fortune. Being young and foolish, I soon spent most of it. I saw then that I must change my ways, and made up my mind to be a merchant. I would travel and do business in foreign lands. So I sold whatever I owned, and used the money to buy a stock of goods.

With a company of other merchants, I set sail on a ship bound for the East Indies. We stopped at many islands, where we bought and sold and traded our goods.

One day the wind died down, and the captain anchored at a beautiful little island.

Passengers and crew alike went ashore. Some brought washtubs and started to wash clothes, some walked about, talking and laughing, and some built fires to cook a meal.

We were all enjoying ourselves, one way or another, when suddenly the earth trembled beneath our feet. The captain had remained on the ship, and now he cried out:

"Ho! Back to the ship! Run for your lives! This is no island, but a great whale. He has been sleeping here so long that grass and trees have grown on him. But your fires have awakened him, and he will plunge into the sea."

Everyone on the island ran toward the ship, but I was too far away to reach it. The whale heaved itself deep into the sea, and huge waves washed over me. I would have drowned, except that, luckily, a wooden washtub came floating by. I leaped into it, just as a breeze sprang up and the ship sailed off without me.

All day I floated in the tub, tossed this way and that by the mighty waves. Night came, and I was sure I would never see the light of morning. But my tub stayed afloat, and the next day, to my great joy, I drifted toward the steep and rocky shore of an island. I climbed up the cliff, lay down under a tree, and fell into a deep sleep.

A few hours later, I was awakened by the sound of hoofbeats. Opening my eyes, I saw a herd of horses grazing around me, and some men on horseback.

"Who are you?" they cried. "Where do you come from? What are you doing here?"

After I had answered their questions, they told me they were the servants of King Mihrjan, who ruled over the island.

"These are the King's horses, too," they said proudly. "We bring them here to graze on the good grass."

They shared their food with me, then gave me a horse and rode with me to the capital city. I was taken to the King, who welcomed me kindly and had me tell him of my adventures.

"Truly, it is a wonder that you are alive," he said. "Stay with us as long as you like."

At the King's orders, I was given clothing and anything else I needed, and my stay on the island was pleasant enough. But I longed to return to Baghdad, and often I went to the port to see if there was a ship that would take me home. And one day, to my delight, I saw the same ship on which I had set out on my voyage.

Hurrying to the captain, I said, "I am Sinbad, and my goods are still aboard your ship."

The captain did not recognize me and glared at me angrily.

"Are there no honest men left in the world?" he said. "With my own eyes I saw Sinbad sink into the sea. And yet you dare to say that you are Sinbad, just to get something that does not belong to you!"

"O Captain," I said, "listen to me, and you will find that I am telling the truth."

I told him everything that had happened, and as I spoke, several merchants on the ship gathered around us.

"This is indeed Sinbad," they said, and at last the captain believed me and gave me my goods.

I chose some of the best of my goods and made a present of them to the King. He gave me valuable gifts in return. I traded the rest of my goods for spices, sandals, and other things of the island country, which I sold at a great profit after returning home on the ship. Once again I was a rich man. I bought houses and land, and lived a life of pleasure and comfort.

But I soon grew tired of being idle. So I set off on my second voyage, with a fine stock of goods to trade and sell. We sailed from city to city, and all went well until we put in at an island where no one lived. Fruit trees grew there, and springs of clear water bubbled up from the rocks, but there was not a sign of a house or a man.

I walked about for a while with some companions from the ship, then lay down under a tree and fell asleep. When I awoke, I called out to my companions. The only answer was the shrill cry of a bird. I rushed to the shore—just in time to see the ship disappearing in the distance. Everyone on board had forgotten about me, and I was alone on a desert island.

At first I wept with rage, blaming myself for having left the pleasures of Baghdad for another dangerous voyage. Then, knowing that rage would not help me, I climbed a tall tree and looked around. At the center of the island, rising above the greenery, I saw a large white dome.

Getting down from the tree, I hurried toward the dome, and found that it was really a huge egg. As I stared at it, the sky suddenly grew dark and a great shadow fell over me. A tremendous bird was flying toward the island. I remembered having heard stories about such a bird, and that it was called a roc.

Now the roc settled on the egg, covered it with its wings, and went to sleep. Quickly I unwound my turban and tied myself to the bird's leg.

"When the roc flies off again," I said to myself, "he will carry me away from this island."

And that is exactly what happened. At dawn the next day, the roc spread its wings and rose high into the air. It flew far from the island to another land, where it came down in a valley.

As soon as we touched the earth, I unbound myself and ran as far as I could. Looking back, I saw the roc flying off, clutching a gigantic serpent in its claws. I

rocks. The merchants frighten the eagles away and take the diamonds."

At once I picked up the biggest diamonds in sight. After stuffing them into my sash, I tied myself to a large piece of meat with my turban. Before long an eagle swooped down and seized the meat in its claws. It carried the meat, and me as well, to its nest on the mountain. Just as I unbound myself there was a loud noise, and the eagle was frightened away.

The merchant who had made the noise came running up, amazed to see me there. When he could find no diamonds sticking to the meat, he began to shout at me for robbing him.

"I am no robber, but an honest merchant," I said. "I have diamonds enough for both of us. Have as many as you like."

Pleased by my words, he took me to the other merchants who were seeking diamonds in the mountains. They were full of wonder at my story, for no man had ever been known to come out of the valley alive. I journeyed with them to a city, where I gave the merchant who had found me his choice

saw, too, that the valley was surrounded by mountains. Their peaks were hidden by clouds, and their rocky sides were too steep to climb.

"What have I done?" I said. "I am worse off here than I was on the island!"

Walking aimlessly about, I discovered diamonds scattered everywhere on the ground, many of them of enormous size. But the valley was swarming with terrible snakes, each big enough to swallow an elephant at one gulp.

I spent the night hiding in a cave. When I came out of it the next morning, a large chunk of meat fell from the mountain and landed near me. A minute later, several more pieces of meat came tumbling from the cliffs. I did not know what to make of this, until I remembered that I had heard of merchants who gathered diamonds in a strange way.

"I never believed those tales before," I thought, "but now I see that they are true. The merchants come to these mountains and throw down chunks of meat, which strike the ground so hard that some diamonds stick to them. Then the eagles carry off the meat to their nests high among the

of my diamonds. He took a few, and the rest I sold for many dinars.

And so at last I returned home, and enjoyed myself in Baghdad for a while. But I soon grew restless, and went off to sea again with another company of merchants.

And a jolly company it was, until a great wind blew our ship into strange waters. Not even the captain knew where we were.

After the wind died down, we made for the nearest island to repair our torn sails. No sooner was the ship anchored than we were attacked by hairy little creatures that looked more like apes than men. Clambering up to the deck, they overcame the crew, forced us ashore, and made off with our ship.

We wandered about the wild, rocky island, and were surprised to find a castle surrounded by a high wall. We went through the open gate into the courtyard, and there we saw some large iron spits for roasting meat. Near the spits was a huge pile of bones.

"These look like human bones," one of the merchants said.

"They are indeed human bones!" roared a loud, harsh voice behind us.

We turned quickly, and saw before us a hideous giant, three times as tall as the tallest man. His teeth were like tusks and his ears hung down to his shoulders. He shut the gate behind him and, reaching out with his huge hand, he picked me up.

"Too lean, too lean," he growled, looking me over carefully.

He let me fall to the ground, and picked up one after another of my companions. But not until he came to the captain was he satisfied.

We lay huddled together while the giant killed the captain, lit a fire, and roasted him on a spit. After eating him, the giant tossed the bones on the pile and went to sleep. All night the air rumbled with his snores. Then, in the morning, he awoke and walked off somewhere, leaving the gate open.

As soon as he was gone, we ran out and roamed over the island. But we could find no place to hide. Afraid that the giant would slaughter us all if he found us outside the walls, we returned to the castle.

At sunset the giant stamped in through the gate, shaking the earth with his foot-steps. Again he chose a man, ate him as he had the captain, and lay down to sleep.

After that we hurried back to the castle, where the giant was still snoring. We took two of the iron spits he used for roasting men, put their ends into the fire, and heated them until they were red-hot. Then the boldest of us picked up the spits and thrust them into the giant's eyes, blinding him.

With a great cry of pain and rage, the giant sprang up. He rushed about the courtyard, reaching for us with his huge hands. But we were able to stay out of his way, and at last, roaring and howling, he found the gate and stumbled away.

We ran at once to the shore where our raft was hidden.

"If there is no sign of the monster by evening, we will know that he is dead," I said. "But if he comes back, we must take to our raft."

While his snores rumbled like thunder, the rest of us gathered together, talking.

"We must kill this monster before he eats us all!" said one of the men.

"Listen to me, O my brothers," I said. "First let us take some of his firewood to the shore and build a raft. If we are not able to kill him, we will try to escape by the sea. It is true that we might all be drowned—but anything is better than being roasted and eaten."

The others agreed to my plan, and we spent most of the night building the raft.

I had hardly spoken when we saw the giant coming toward us, with two others even uglier than himself. We rushed to our raft, but the giants threw huge rocks and many of our men fell dead. The rest of us paddled the raft as fast as we could and escaped to the open sea.

As we drifted helplessly among the great jagged waves, several of our men lost their hold on the raft and were washed overboard. Only three of us were alive when we reached another island. How thankful we were as we wearily dragged ourselves up the shore and lay down to rest!

But there were still more terrors ahead of us. Even as we lay there, an enormous serpent came slithering up. Before we could get to our feet, it swallowed one of my companions whole and crawled away.

That night, trying to escape the serpent, my lone companion and I climbed up a tree. To our horror, the serpent followed us. Reaching my companion first, it swallowed him, then quickly slid away. And I knew that unless I could think of some way to save myself, the serpent would be back and swallow me.

Working with all the strength I had left, I tore loose the boards of the raft. I took some tough vines and bound one board crosswise at my head, another at my feet, another at my shoulders, one across the waistline, and one at my knees.

When the serpent came gliding up again, I stretched myself on the ground. All through that horrible night it tried to swallow me, but the boards kept it from getting at me.

At daybreak the serpent crawled away, hissing angrily. I untied myself and hurried to the shore, where I saw a ship passing by. Breaking off the branch of a tree, I waved it and shouted as loud as I could. To my great joy, I saw a boat being lowered, and knew that I was saved.

Once I was aboard the vessel, I told the captain my adventures since my ship had been captured.

"This is strange," he said. "In our voyage among the islands, we came upon a ship that was adrift. Her cargo was untouched, and we put it aboard our own ship. If any of it is yours, you are welcome to take it, for we do not want anything that belongs to another."

I followed the captain into the hold of the ship, and there indeed were my goods. I continued on my voyage, a thankful man, and by the time I returned to Baghdad I had greatly increased my wealth.

Happy and rich as I was, I could not stay away from the sea. Not for nothing was I called Sinbad the Sailor. I sailed away again and again, and on one of my voyages I had to escape from ferocious cannibals who ate human flesh.

On another voyage I came to the island of Sarandib, which abounds in rubies and precious stones. In that beautiful land, when the Sultan leaves his palace, he sits on a throne mounted on an elephant. Before him, also riding on elephants, go a thousand men,

each of them dressed in cloth of gold.

On still another voyage, I found the Ivory Hill—a great mound of the bones and tusks of elephants, which come here to die.

But I would like to tell you now of the voyage on which I met with the Old Man of the Sea. This time I sailed on a fine ship of my own, taking with me several other merchants.

We traveled from city to city, trading in each, then put in at an unknown island in the open sea. On the island we found an enormous roc's egg. It seemed ready to hatch, for the bill of the young roc had already cracked the shell.

"I have heard that a young roc is good eating," one of the merchants said. "Let us have a feast."

"No, no! Do not touch the egg!" I said. But the merchants only laughed at my fears. Cracking the egg, they took out the young roc, cut it into pieces, and roasted them over a fire. Just as they finished eating, two rocs appeared in the sky, their wings blotting out the sun. When they saw the broken egg, the great birds raised a cry louder than thunder.

"We must leave before we are destroyed!" I shouted, and we quickly boarded the ship.

We hauled in our anchor and sailed away from the island, and the rocs flew off. They were soon back, circling over the ship. Each of them carried a huge boulder in its claws. With a terrible cry, they dropped their boulders on the ship, which smashed into countless bits.

I was thrown into the water, and to keep from drowning I grasped a plank that had sprung from the ship. The waves carried me swiftly away. Clinging to the plank, I floated

with his hands for me to carry him across the stream on my back. Thinking that he badly needed help, I did as he wished. I stopped at the place to which he had pointed, and stooped so that he could get down. Instead, he clasped his legs so tightly around my neck that I fell down in a faint.

Even then, the old man did not let go. He kicked me with his heels, so hard that I was forced to get up. He pointed to the trees with the best fruit, and I had to carry him there. I tried to shake him off, but his strength was unbelievably great. And if I refused to do as he asked, or walked too slowly, he kicked me until I felt as though I had been beaten with whips. At night, when we lay down to sleep, he kept his legs wound tightly around my neck. In the morning I was awakened by his kicks and forced to carry him about again.

This went on for weeks, until I began to feel that I would never be rid of him. Then one day I picked up a gourd that had fallen from a tree. I scooped out the inside, gathered some grapes, and filled the gourd with their juice. I left it in the sun for some days, and the juice turned into excellent wine. Every once in a while I would refresh myself by taking a drink, and I began to feel a little more cheerful.

on the sea until I was cast up on the shore of an island.

Hungry, thirsty, tired and terrified, I was more dead than alive. I looked around and saw that the island was like a garden of many delights. There were trees bearing ripe fruit, streams of sweet water, bright flowers and twittering birds. I ate and drank, then lay down in the grass and slept.

When I awoke, it was morning. Feeling greatly refreshed, I walked about, and came to a broad stream of running water. And there, sitting on the bank, was an old man. He was thin and bent, and naked except for a cloth around his waist.

I greeted him eagerly, but he said not a word. He only moaned, and made signs

68

The old man noticed this, and signalled for me to give him the gourd. He put it to his lips, tasted the wine, then drank it to the last drop. Soon he began to sway, and his grip on me became looser. Stooping over suddenly, I threw him to the ground, where he lay without moving.

Thankful to be rid of him at last, I ran down to the shore. I almost wept with joy, for a ship had anchored at the island to take on fresh water. The men of the ship crowded around me and asked how I came to be here. They shook their heads wonderingly, amazed at what I told them.

"The old man who rode on your shoulders is called the Old Man of the Sea," they said. "And never before has anyone escaped from him alive!"

I sailed on the ship to the City of Apes, and there I said good-by to the ship's company. They were off on a long voyage that would take them far from my home.

Now this City of Apes that I found myself in was a strange place. All the houses faced the sea, and the people spent every night on boats and ships anchored off shore. The reason was that, as soon as darkness fell, the apes came down from the hills. They overran the city, and would kill anyone foolish enough to linger there. In the morning the apes went back to the hills, and the people returned to their homes.

I was sitting on the beach, miserable and lonely, when a man came up to me.

"I see you are a stranger," he said. "Have you any way of earning a living?"

"No," I answered. "I was a rich merchant, with a ship of my own and a fine cargo of goods. But my ship went down in the ocean, and everyone was drowned but me."

"Then take this," he said, handing me a large sack of cloth. "Fill it with pebbles, and I will show you how to earn a living."

I wondered how I could earn my living with pebbles, but I kept my thoughts to myself. I thanked the man for his kindness, and we joined some other men who were picking up pebbles on the beach.

When our sacks were full, we journeyed into the hills until we came to a great forest of coco palms. We threw the pebbles at the apes, which were asleep high in the trees. Chattering angrily, they plucked coconuts from the trees and threw them down at us. We filled our sacks with the coconuts and went back to the city, where we sold them.

For some time I gathered coconuts every day, and, with the help and advice of my new friend, earned a large sum of money. When at last a ship came in that would take me home, I bought a large stock of goods and took it with me on the voyage. I traded at various places, and reached Baghdad much richer than I had been before.

And so ended the story that Sinbad the Sailor told to the porter, as they sat eating in the magnificent house.

"Seven voyages I made in all," Sinbad said. "And then I decided to stay here and go to sea no more."

"Truly, O Sinbad, you have suffered much and lived through many dangers," the porter said. "May you long enjoy your wealth."

Sinbad then gave the porter a gift of money—one hundred sequins for each of his seven voyages—and after that the two were the best of friends.

The Man Who Never Laughed

THE Caliph Haroun al-Raschid sat one afternoon in the courtyard of his palace, sipping sweet black coffee and smoking his hookah. Feeling deeply contented, he looked about him and smiled. How comfortable he was! How beautiful was this courtyard with its tinkling fountain! How pleasant to be surrounded by faithful courtiers and servants! How good to know that there was peace and plenty in the land!

At last he spoke his thoughts aloud to his Grand Vizier. "It is good to be alive in our land at this time. Surely, there is not a man among us who has no cause to smile. Some may be richer than others, and some may be poorer, but all are happy."

"Truly, it should be as you say, Your Majesty," the Grand Vizier said. "But I know of one man living close to the palace

who is called the man who never laughs—and, indeed, he never does."

"Bring that man to me at once," ordered the Caliph. "We will learn the cause of his sorrow and help him find happiness."

And so the man was brought to the palace. To the Caliph's astonishment, he was handsome and sturdy, and dressed in the finest of robes. But his face was sad and a shadow of gloom seemed to hang over him.

"I hear, worthy sir," the Caliph said, "that you never laugh. What is the reason for your sorrow? Tell us, and we will help you find happiness again."

"The Caliph is a true friend of his people," the sad man said. "But I do not think that even he will be able to help me. Nevertheless, it might interest Your Majesty to hear my story."

The Caliph nodded. "Do tell us your story, and we will see if your sorrow is really beyond help."

And the good Caliph leaned back on his couch, took a puff on his hookah, and prepared to listen.

"I was the only son of a very rich man," the gloomy one began. "I was brought up in luxury and had nothing to do but amuse myself. When my father died suddenly, I spent a year mourning for him. But after that I went back to my idle ways, wasting money on all sorts of foolishness. My father had left all his fortune to me, and I had many friends who were only too glad to help me spend it. In three years my money was gone, and so were my friends. I was forced to beg for work in the market place."

The Caliph Haroun al-Raschid interrupted him. "If it is suitable work that you need, we can easily find it for you. Then you will be happy with the rest of us."

"Hear me out, O Caliph," the sad man said. "For my story is just beginning, and I have not yet come to even the first hint of my trouble."

The Caliph motioned for him to continue, and the man who never laughed went on with his story:

After I had spent all my fortune, I was in the market place one day, asking each passer-by for work, when a solemn-looking, elderly man came up to me.

"Young man," he said, "your face, your hands, and your manner show that you are of gentle birth. You are used to riches, are you not?"

"Indeed I am," I answered. "I am the son of a rich man and have foolishly squandered his wealth. Oh, if only I could have another chance. . . ."

"You can have another chance," the elderly man said, "if you promise to live wisely and honorably."

"I promise—with all my heart!"

My new friend then took me to his home. After a luxurious bath, I was given fresh garments of the finest linen, and my duties were explained to me. Besides my employer, nine other old men lived in the house, and I would be in charge of the household. I was to buy everything necessary, and manage the servants. To pay for all this, I was given a chest containing thirty thousand dinars.

"One thing I must ask you never to do," my employer said. "Never ask why we are so sad and silent—and why we weep."

I promised, and soon I was so accustomed to this strange household it was as if I had lived here all my life. Several years passed, and one of the old men died. Then another died, and still another, until at last only my first employer was left. And when he, too, was on his deathbed, I spoke to him.

"Dear friend," I said, "I have served you and your companions well and faithfully. May I now ask a favor of you?"

"Ask it, my son, and it shall be granted. For you have indeed been faithful to me and my friends, and I am grateful."

"Then tell me why you and your friends always wore mourning, and why you never smiled, and why you wept every day."

The dying man sighed. "Ah, my son, I wish you had not asked me that. My answer may be the beginning of your own misfortune. But it may be that you are destined to know. If you really want to learn the cause of our misery, seek it by opening the door behind the tapestry." And with his bony hand he gestured toward the other part of the house.

Not many days afterward, the old man died, and I became the owner of the house and the riches in it. I had learned to like a quiet life, so that at first I was content to go on living as I had.

But as the weeks went by, I grew restless, and thought of the mysterious door. I wandered from room to room, searching until I found a small door hidden behind a hanging. It was locked with four locks.

I turned away, not wishing to break open the locks. But I returned to the door day after day, gazing at it and knowing that, sooner or later, I would force it open. And one day I did.

The door swung open on a long corridor that seemed to have no end. I started walking down it. After I had walked for about an hour and the end of the corridor was still not in sight, I became frightened and ran.

How long I ran I cannot tell. But suddenly, when I had become too tired to go on, I found myself out of the corridor and on a beach at the edge of the ocean.

I stared at the water, thinking, "I never knew the ocean was so near."

As I walked on the sand, watching the great waves rolling in to shore, an eagle circled high in the air above me. All at once it dropped straight down, seized me in its claws, and flew off over the sea. Although there was only the empty sky above and tossing water below, I felt strangely safe in the grip of the huge bird. At last I was set down on a small island.

Wondering what would happen next, I saw a ship approaching, moving swiftly with the wind. When it came close, I could see that the sails were silk, each of a different color—purple, saffron, crimson, emerald. And when the ship came closer still,

I saw that the crew were young and beautiful maidens in the garb of princesses, their hair blowing in the wind.

A boat was lowered and several of the maidens rowed it to shore. Smiling, they called gently to me in their sweet voices, and took me to the ship. Here I was given magnificent robes and served with delicious foods, while the maidens sailed the ship across the water. Through the rest of that day we sailed, and all the night, and the next day.

Just as the sun began to go down, we drew near a shore that was crowded with people shouting and waving banners. The maidens went ashore with me in their midst, and from every side I heard the cry:

"The bridegroom! Welcome to the bridegroom!"

A guard of mounted soldiers in splendid uniforms brought a horse for me, and we rode to a palace that was rosy in the glow of the setting sun. A radiantly beautiful queen came forth to meet me. And when she led me to a throne next to her own, I felt as though I were in a dream.

The Queen said tenderly, "At last you have come, my bridegroom, as it has been foretold! We shall be married at once. The wedding feast is ready."

Her words filled me with joy, for at first sight of the lovely Queen I had fallen in love with her. I could have wished for nothing better than to marry her and live the rest of my life beside her.

After the marriage ceremony, the Queen said, "You are now king of a peaceful and prosperous land. Everything I own is now yours as well, and you may command any person to carry out your slightest desire. But one thing I must deny you. Do not open this door, or you will bring misfortune and ruin upon yourself."

And she pointed to a small door in the far corner of the room.

For seven years I knew happiness such as is enjoyed by few men on this earth. I was untouched by even a hint of gloom. I almost forgot that there was anything else in life but love and joy and laughter.

Then one day, while the Queen was away on a royal mission, I happened to pass by the forbidden door. I could not help wondering why I had been warned never to open it. How could anything that lay beyond it be dangerous to me, who was master of everything in this land? Surely the Queen was making much of a trifle. I would open the door and show her—and myself—that I had nothing to fear.

Reaching out my hand, I boldly turned the knob. The door swung open, I stepped over the threshold—and the door clanged shut behind me. Once again I found myself on a beach at the edge of the ocean. A huge eagle flew over me, shrieking. It swooped down, clutched me in its claws, and carried me off. After a swift journey over the stormy ocean, it cast me down outside the corridor leading to my own house.

At this point in his story, the man who never laughed was so overcome by grief that he had to stop. The Caliph and his court waited in silence. Then, with tears in his eyes, the man went on with his story.

"For days I wandered on the beach," he said, "crying and calling to my beloved wife. I called to the eagle, too, begging it to come back and take me to the Queen. At last I realized that I would never return to her. Slowly I went through the corridor and into my house. Now I knew the old men's secret, and I understood why they wept. And I saw that I, too, would pass the rest of my days in sorrow."

Again the court was silent as he covered his face with his hands and sobbed.

Then the Caliph spoke. "O unfortunate one, it is plain that I can do nothing to lift the black cloud under which you live. Yet I feel that your lot is not really miserable. You have riches, a fine house, a wealth of memories, and the will to weep. If I tried to remove the cause of your sorrow, I might ruin your life completely.

"Go home, then, and mourn as you have been doing. As for me, I shall remember that I must not be vain and believe that everyone in our land is happy. For now I know that there is at least one man who never laughs."

The Serpent Queen

MANY, MANY years ago, there lived in Greece a wise young scholar by the name of Daniel. So great was his knowledge and so wonderful was his wisdom that word of him spread to other lands, even to far-off Persia. And one day Daniel received a message from the Emperor of Persia, inviting him to come and live in the royal palace and be one of the Emperor's counselors.

Daniel was happy to accept the invitation. He gathered up the thousands of scrolls and manuscripts in his library, and packed them in huge chests. Then, with the chests, he and his wife boarded a ship and sailed for Persia.

The voyage turned out to be an unfortunate one, for the ship was attacked by pirates. After taking the gold and silver in the hold and making the passengers their prisoners, the pirates set fire to the ship.

Daniel pleaded with them to save his chests of precious scrolls and manuscripts. The pirates only laughed. What a strange fellow—valuing words more than gold! But the captain took pity on Daniel and his wife. In the dead of night he set them down unharmed on the coast of Lydia.

In a strange land, and saddened by the loss of his library, Daniel soon became ill. He had himself propped up in bed and began to put down the best of the teachings of human wisdom. He was so fine a scholar that he was able to do this in five closely-written pages.

Meanwhile, his wife bore a son, who was called Hasib. Daniel worked even harder at his writing, fighting to keep alive until he had finished. And when he had set down the final word, he called weakly to his wife.

"I have nothing to leave my son except these five pages," he said. "Give them to our child with my blessing, when he is ready to understand them. Forgive me, my dear wife, for failing you now, but I cannot go on living. I know that my end is near."

He kissed her tenderly, and they both wept. Then he lay back and quietly stopped breathing.

And so Daniel's wife was left to bring up Hasib alone. At the boy's birth, the stars had foretold that he would become one of the world's wisest men, if only he would live through a terrible danger in his youth. Hasib's mother knew this, and watched over him carefully.

But all through his childhood, Hasib showed no signs of wisdom, nor did he care to be a scholar. He grew to be a young man without even learning to read or write. His mother sent him out with the woodcutters, so that he could at least start to earn a living. Hasib was strong and eager, and soon became a good worker.

One day, while the woodcutters were in the forest, a great storm suddenly swept down upon them. They all ran to a nearby cave, where they waited for the rain to stop. Hasib happened to sit a little away from the others, deeper within the cave.

Without thinking, he tapped the ground beside him lightly with his axe handle. It made a strange sound. Curious, Hasib scraped away the soil with his bare hands, and saw a slab of stone with an iron ring fastened to it.

The young man got to his feet, bent

down, and grasped the ring with both hands. He pulled with all his strength until he lifted the stone, revealing a deep, dark well in the earth.

By this time, the other woodcutters had noticed what Hasib was doing. Crowding around him, they lit a candle and thrust it into the well. To their astonishment, they saw that it was very deep and lined with honeycomb. Hasib reached down and broke off a piece. When he tasted it, he found it contained the most fragrant, delicious honey he had ever eaten.

Each of the woodcutters then had a taste. They began to talk excitedly, agreeing that this discovery would make them rich. Here at their very feet was a treasure—an endless store of honey, waiting to be gathered and sold. No longer would they have to earn a miserable living by chopping down trees.

Hasib listened, amazed, for they had left him completely out of their plans.

"But was it not I who discovered the honey in the first place?" he asked timidly. "I am sure some people would say that by right all of the honey belongs to me."

The woodcutters stared at him, but did not answer. Instead, they moved aside and talked among themselves in low voices. Then, smiling in a friendly way, they turned back to Hasib. They asked him to look into the well and see how far down it was lined with honeycomb.

As Hasib knelt and peered over the rim of the well, one of the men gave him a push. Before Hasib could even cry out, down he went into the well, falling for what seemed to be a long time. At last he landed on ground that was soft with velvety moss.

From far above, Hasib heard the men loosening honeycomb from the wall. Then he heard the slab of stone fall heavily into place. He knew there was no use calling for help. He could only sit there, unhurt from the fall, but stunned by the way the woodcutters had turned against him.

After a while, he felt something crawling on the back of his left hand. His eyes were now used to the gloom, and he saw that the crawling thing was a spider. Without thinking, he crushed it to death.

And then he asked himself, "Where did that spider come from?"

Looking carefully around he noticed some cracks in the stone walls that hemmed him in. He took his knife from his belt and pried at one of the cracks. A piece of rock loosened and fell from the wall. He crawled through the space left by the rock, and found himself in a narrow passage.

Hasib crept along on hands and knees until he came to an iron door. It was fastened with a silver lock, in which was a gold key. Turning the key, he pushed open the door—and almost fainted with fright.

Before him was a vast cavern, filled with something that moved and glistened like water—and yet Hasib knew that it was not water. All about were low, golden stools, and coiled on each stool was a serpent, its eyes like emeralds. Near Hasib stood a throne of gold and jasper and precious stones. He scrambled up on it, staring at the serpents on the stools. When he took his eyes off them, he saw that what looked like water was a mass of serpents, thousands and thousands of them.

Surrounded by the hissing, coiling serpents, Hasib perched on the throne, shivering with terror. Then a most enormous serpent appeared, carrying a gold platter on its head. On the platter lay another serpent, and as Hasib looked at it he lost his fear, for it had the face of a woman, with kind, sad eyes and a lovely mouth.

"Fear nothing, young man," the serpent said in a low, sweet voice. "I am the Queen of the Serpents, and it has been foretold that you would come here."

Hasib started to move off the throne, but the Queen stopped him.

"Stay where you are, my friend," she said. "I will rest among my subjects."

She slid off the golden platter to one of the stools. When she had settled herself, she asked Hasib whether he was hungry.

"Indeed I am," he said. "My adventures have made me lose track of time, but I am sure that I have not eaten for many hours—perhaps for several days."

The Queen ordered food to be brought for Hasib, and he ate and drank from gold vessels encrusted with jewels. He felt his strength return, and wished only to be led back into the light so that he could find his way home.

"Now that you are refreshed," the Queen said in her sweet voice, "perhaps you will tell me your story. Tell me who you are, and what brought you here."

Although he was impatient to be gone, Hasib courteously told the Queen everything that had happened to him.

After he had finished his tale, the Queen said, "Now I will tell you my story."

Again Hasib had to be polite, and he sat quietly while the Queen spoke. But he was so eager to be off, he scarcely heard what she said. The Queen's story was a long one, and she stopped now and then for Hasib to eat or sleep. And each time she continued where she left off.

At last Hasib could stand it no longer. Falling upon his knees before the strange,

beautiful creature, he said, "Your Majesty, I beg of you not to keep me here longer. I am sick for home."

"I know, I know," said the Queen softly. "By keeping you here, I was only trying to put off the day of my death."

"How can my return home lead to your death?" asked Hasib, greatly troubled.

The Queen sighed. "Ah, poor youth, it is not your doing. I shall torture you no longer. You may leave now—but promise me one thing."

"Anything in my power, good Queen!"

"Do not go to the public bath," the Queen said.

Hasib promised, wondering why she had made such a strange request. But he had little time to think about it, for the Queen was showing him the way out. She led the

way through countless dark corridors and winding passages until, suddenly, Hasib was out in the light of day.

"Go now, dear friend," said the Queen, "and remember your promise. But do not be sorrowful if you do not keep it. For it is foretold that I shall die because of you, and truly there is little we can do to change what is foretold."

Hasib watched her as she disappeared into the cavern from which they had just come forth. Then he glanced about him, and knew at once in what part of the forest he was.

Before long he was back in his own village, where his joyful mother threw her arms around him. She laughed and cried, as if she did not know which she wanted to do most. Hasib understood why when he learned, to his great amazement, that he had been gone for two years.

News of Hasib's return quickly spread, and the men who had pushed him down the well came running to see him. They had long ago become sorry that they had done such a cruel deed, and had cared for Hasib's mother while he was gone. The great store of honey in the well had made them rich, and now they were all successful merchants. They offered Hasib half of their riches, and he gladly accepted.

His mother was happy to see that her son had grown much more manly and sensible. Still, she often sighed as she thought of her husband Daniel, the great scholar, and his five pages of wisdom. She knew that Hasib was not yet ready for them.

But Hasib himself knew nothing of this. With his new wealth he became a merchant, built a house, and was soon married. He had many friends. One morning some of them asked him to go bathing in the public bath.

"Come, Hasib!" they said. "You have never seen our splendid black marble bathing pool!"

Forgetting the warning of the Serpent Queen, Hasib threw his cloak around him and joined his friends. Singing merrily, they went to the bath. But hardly had he dipped his body in the water, when he was roughly pulled out by two strangers.

"This is the man!" they cried. "See, his skin has turned black!"

Everyone looked at Hasib. His skin had indeed turned black in the clear water of the pool. He was made to dress and was taken to the inn, where the Grand Vizier of the Emperor of Persia sat with a great scroll open before him.

Hasib spoke out boldly, trying to hide his fear.

"I demand that you let me go!" he said. "Dragging an innocent man away from his friends like a criminal!"

But the two men who had seized him said to the Vizier, "Here he is, Your Highness. His skin turned black the moment he entered the water."

The Vizier looked at Hasib coldly.

"I am sorry to trouble you, young man," he said. "But you will soon understand why you were brought here. The Emperor Kerezan of Persia has a terrible illness. His doctors say that he will die—unless he eats of the Queen of the Serpents. No one knew where to seek this creature until we searched through all the books of magic, spells, and prophecy. We found the answer in this scroll."

He held out the scroll to Hasib, who read:

"There is a man who will spend two years in the realm of the serpents. Then he will come forth again and return to his home. He will be known when he goes to the public bath and his skin turns black."

"You are that man!" the Vizier cried. "Lead us to the Queen of the Serpents!"

Hasib could have wept for his forgetfulness. He had broken his promise to the gentle creature who had befriended him, and now she must die. At first he refused to show the Vizier where she was. But he was beaten until he was forced to obey. Sadly he led the Vizier to the cave where he had first discovered the well of honey.

Going down into the well, the Persians captured the Serpent Queen. They put her in a cage and set out at once for Persia, taking the unwilling Hasib with them. The night before they arrived, the Serpent Queen spoke secretly to Hasib.

"We shall be taken to the Vizier's house, my poor friend," she said. "There he will ask you to kill me and divide my body into three parts. You must refuse, and make him do it himself. He will then put each of the three parts into separate pots to cook.

86

"While the pots are on the fire, he will be summoned to the Emperor. He will ask you to tend the pots while he is gone. When the cooking is done, each pot will yield one small flask of clear liquid. The Vizier will tell you to save the liquid from the first part for him, to cure him of an illness. The liquid from the second part he will say is for the Emperor. He will offer you the third flask as your reward. Instead of doing as he asks, make sure you drink the first flask and leave the third for him."

Hasib obeyed the Serpent Queen, and everything happened as she had said. But when he drank the first flask of liquid, a great change came over him. Suddenly he was filled with great understanding and saw the world with a new wisdom.

When the Vizier returned and asked for his flask, Hasib gave him the third. Swallowing the contents in a gulp, the Vizier fell to the floor and died. The liquid was a poison with which the wicked man had meant to destroy Hasib.

Now Hasib took the second flask of liquid to the dying Emperor Kerezan. No sooner had the Emperor swallowed it, than his health returned. He sat up and looked gratefully at Hasib.

"What is your name and where do you come from, honored sir?" the Emperor asked.

"I am Hasib, the son of Daniel, the famous Greek scholar. He died when I was still a baby."

At once a smile of joy lit up the face of the Emperor.

"Many years ago," he said, "your father disappeared while on the way to my kingdom. I see that you, too, are a scholar and follow in his footsteps. May I invite you and your family to come and live with me here in my palace? You will guide me and advise me on my royal duties."

Hasib agreed, and sent for his wife, his mother, his servants, and his household goods. This time no pirates looted the ship, and before long Hasib and his family were together again. As soon as his mother saw him, she knew that wisdom had come to her son. She took the five pages Daniel had written out of a secret box.

"Here at last is your inheritance, my son," she said. "Now I know that you are worthy of it."

And truly it was so, for Hasib became the Grand Vizier of Persia, and for many years the people of the land were made happy by his wisdom and good deeds.

The Poor Man's Dream

In Baghdad there lived a man who thought himself the most unfortunate person on earth. To begin with, he could find no work. He had become so poor that he could not even afford to rent a hovel. He had to move his family into an old, crumbling ruin that lay outside the wall of the city.

On top of this, he had a wife who never spoke a kind word to him. True, her tongue had been made sharper by hunger. But it did seem that she was always complaining, always scolding, always telling him that he was lazy and worthless and would never amount to anything.

"The trouble with you," she would say in her shrill voice, "is that you have no more ambition than that dried-up fountain falling to pieces in our courtyard. You have no wish to be anything but a poor man! You enjoy it! You don't care how much your wife and children suffer!"

But worst of all his misfortunes was a dream that came to the poor man, night after night, whenever he lay down to sleep. In his dream he would find himself on a wide plain. He would be walking, walking, walking under an empty sky. On his back was a heavy pack. And a voice kept roaring into his ear:

"On to Cairo! On to Cairo! Your fortune is in Cairo!"

The walking was so hard, the voice so loud and terrible, that he would wake up panting, as tired as when he had lain down, and full of fear.

He told his wife about the dream and said, "Perhaps I really should go to Cairo."

"Cairo!" she mocked. "Do you know how far it is? And you would have to walk all the way! Besides—" and she looked at

him through narrowed eyes—"how do I know you will really go to Cairo? And if you do, how do I know if you will ever get back? You are just lazy and mean enough to run away and leave me to starve with our little ones! Cairo, indeed!"

And so the man said no more about Cairo. But he went on dreaming his dream.

Now, there was a well of good, clear water not far from the ruin where he lived. Often he would sit at the well, waiting for passing travelers to come along. When they stopped to draw water, he would ask them if they had any work to be done. In this way, he was sometimes able to earn a few coins.

One day, as he was sitting in his usual place, a great caravan stopped at the well. The men watered their camels and donkeys, drew water for themselves, and chatted about the journey yet before them. It turned out that they were going to Cairo.

Cairo! The man arose and came closer to the travelers. He asked if they had any work he could do. He could make himself useful if they would let him join them on their journey.

"Come along and welcome!" they cried. "You can ride on one of the pack camels."

The man hastened to climb upon one of the kneeling beasts before it lurched to its feet. Bending over so that his wife could not spy him as the caravan rode by, he left the city of Baghdad. That night he slept with the men and the animals under the stars. It was the first night in many, many weeks that he did not dream.

He went on with the caravan, until at last he saw the towers of Cairo, shining in the sunset. The caravan broke up as soon as it arrived in the city, and by the time darkness fell, the man was alone. He had no money for food and no place to sleep. He wandered through the strange streets until he was too weary to walk any farther. Then he sank down in a doorway, let his eyes close, and fell asleep.

He was awakened at dawn by a rough hand shaking his shoulder, and a voice saying, "We have beggars enough of our own in Cairo. We don't need you. Now come along! And hurry!"

He was pushed and pulled through the streets and thrown on a pile of straw in a prison. There he lay, frightened and hungry, his limbs trembling and his teeth chattering. After many hours, he was dragged before a judge.

The judge looked down upon him sternly from his high seat. "Tell me, from what city do you come?"

"Baghdad, O Protector of the Poor."

"Indeed. And how did you get here?" asked the judge.

"With a caravan," the poor man said.

"And why did you make the journey?"

"This may seem strange and foolish to you, O Learned One," replied the man humbly. "But I came to Cairo because of a dream I had every night, telling me that I would make my fortune here. And instead of making my fortune, I am thrown into jail like a thief!"

He lowered his head in shame, almost ready to burst into tears.

The judge was a merciful man. "Now, now," he said, "things are not as bad as they seem. You have made yourself no poorer by coming to Cairo than you were in Baghdad. Here is half a dinar. Buy something to eat, then be off and on your way home."

The man took the coin and thanked the judge. "But how am I to get back home?" he said.

"Be thankful that I am allowing you to go free," the judge said severely. "Here in Cairo we usually put beggars and vagabonds in jail and forget about them. I have been merciful to you because you have answered my questions honestly. Besides, I am sorry for you because you let yourself be fooled by a false dream."

The judge paused and looked at the man. "Shall I tell you something really amusing? I, too, have a dream every night, but I am not so foolish as to believe in it."

"May I ask what that dream is?" the poor man said—not because he was at all curious, but because it seemed the polite thing to say.

"Judge for yourself how foolish a dream it is. In my dream I am alone, all alone. I am outside the city of Baghdad, near a broken, unused fountain standing in the courtyard of a miserable ruin."

The man's heart began to beat faster when he heard these words.

"As I stand there by the fountain," the judge went on, "I hear a voice. 'Dig!' it says. 'Dig down behind that loose stone. A treasure is hidden there. He who digs for it will find it.' Now if I were as foolish as you, I would leave my home and go off to Baghdad with a spade on my shoulder, look-ing stupidly for old, dried-up fountains."

The judge threw back his head, laughing so heartily that his back teeth showed. The man laughed, too. He tried to keep his laughter from showing the wild, crazy joy he felt.

"Farewell! And may the road back to Baghdad be a pleasant one," the judge said.

"Thank you," the man said.

His trip back to Baghdad seemed much shorter than his trip to Cairo, even though he walked most of the way. Once in a while some kind, good-natured traveler would let him ride a pack animal.

It was night when he arrived at the ruin where he made his home. A white moon shed its light on the courtyard and the old, dry fountain.

The man wasted no time in looking for the loose stone. With his bare hands he moved it and began clawing away the earth where the stone had rested. It broke in clods as dry as salt. He dug a little more—and then he found a leather saddlebag, heavy with treasure! He tore the bag open, and rubies, diamonds, pearls and emeralds shimmered in the moonlight. The man wanted to laugh—to laugh as loud as the judge had done in Cairo. But he held himself back, not wanting to wake his wife.

He put the bag of treasure under the ragged rug on which he slept, and lay down. In the morning he was awakened by the shrill voice of his wife. He looked up at her as she stood over him, her hands on her hips.

"Well, well!" she said. "So you've turned up again! And where have you been, if I may ask?"

"To Cairo."

"And I suppose you found our fortune, as the dream foretold," the woman said.

"Yes, I did," said the man, and took the saddlebag out from under the rug.

His wife stared into the open mouth of the bag, so astonished that she could not say another word all day.

And from that time on, the poor man knew nothing but good fortune. He was poor no longer, and moved his family to a fine house. At night his sleep was untroubled by dreams. And best of all, his wife no longer scolded or complained, but always spoke to him politely, and with the greatest respect.

92